All she wanted was Noah

And she could be exactly what he'd been searching for—a woman who shared his passions, but would walk away in the morning. No matter how hard it was. She loved him that much.

"Miranda, you don't know what you're saying," Noah said, obviously trying to gain control of the situation. "You're not a love-'em-and-leave-'em kind of girl."

"No, Noah, I'm not. I'm not a *girl* at all—good or otherwise. I'm a woman who's pretty damn certain of what I want." She moved over to rub her head against his chest. "All I'm asking for is one night, maybe two. You, me—" the sound of her voice, so throaty, deep and insistent, lured him to relax "—and the storm."

She pushed the gossamer fabric aside, peeling it away from her body like a layer of translucent skin. Then she reached out and cupped his chin, splaying her fingers along his cheek before combing them through his hair. "Sometimes, Noah, good girls do." Raising herself on her knees, Miranda leaned forward and buried her lips in his neck. *And they do it very well...."*

Dear Reader,

I wish I could be provocative and say that since I *wasn't* a good girl myself, I settled for *writing* about one. But that would be a great big fib. Even though I write ultra-sexy romance novels, my values are decidedly traditional. Stop snickering. They are! There's something incredibly erotic about knowing that once you find the right man, you'll be enjoying him—and vice versa—for the rest of your life.

The heroines in my previous books, #686 *Seducing Sullivan* and #724 *Private Lessons,* were both a bit cynical about love, marriage and men in general. Since I'm always looking for a different approach to my stories, endlessly scientific Miranda Carpenter sprang to life. She's an expert on sex, but her knowledge is book learned and theory based. She's been saving firsthand experience for Mr. Right—though she's conveniently avoided looking for the guy. She never expects the man of her dreams to crash her lecture and question her credibility.

I love to hear from die-hard romantics like me. And if you once were or still are (or better yet, wish you could have been) a "good girl," then I'd really like to hear what you think. Write to me at Box 270885, Tampa, FL 33688-0885 or link to my page by visiting Harlequin's exciting new Web site at eHarlequin.com.

Sincerely,

Julie Elizabeth Leto

GOOD GIRLS DO!
Julie Elizabeth Leto

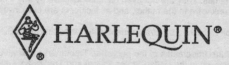

TORONTO • NEW YORK • LONDON
AMSTERDAM • PARIS • SYDNEY • HAMBURG
STOCKHOLM • ATHENS • TOKYO • MILAN • MADRID
PRAGUE • WARSAW • BUDAPEST • AUCKLAND

For Mom and Dad
Being a "good girl" isn't so hard when parents
give love and support like you do. You win "The Most
Phenomenal Parents on Earth" contest—hands down.

And to Janelle and Karen...
Are you sure we haven't known each other since
kindergarten? Thanks for keeping me grounded
and sane. Divas rule.

ISBN 0-373-25883-6

GOOD GIRLS DO!

Copyright © 2000 by Julie Leto Klapka.

This edition published by arrangement with Harlequin Books S.A.

® and TM are trademarks of the publisher. Trademarks indicated with
® are registered in the United States Patent and Trademark Office, the
Canadian Trade Marks Office and in other countries.

Visit us at www.eHarlequin.com

Printed in U.S.A.

_____ Prologue _____

May 1, 2000

Dr. Miranda Carpenter, Ph.D.
Science Department
University of Southern Florida
Tampa, Florida 33620

Dear Dr. Carpenter,

The Campus Institute for Safe Sex (C.I.S.S.) is proud to announce your nomination for the Most Virtuous Woman on Campus award. You have always been a strong supporter of our group and our goal to disseminate accurate information about sex to the student body. We could think of no better way to honor your commitment, both personal and professional, to virtuous and wholesome living.

Ms. Teri Carpenter of the Drama Department submitted the initial nomination, which was seconded by Dr. Noah Yeager, your colleague in the Department of Psychology. You are competing with five other nominees, one from each academic class including the graduate program.

The contest, a precursor to Sexual Awareness

Week, will entail the "supervision" of a date with the man of your choice. A reporter from the campus newspaper will be the observer and will then publish a summary so students may judge which candidate conducted herself in the most virtuous manner.

If, for some reason, you can't think of anyone you'd like to take on this date, we've already heard from several volunteers. The winner will be announced at our C.I.S.S. Week kick-off rally.

Sincerely,
C.I.S.S.

Cc: Ms. Teri Carpenter
Dr. Noah Yeager

UH-OH.

Noah Yeager skimmed the letter on his desk again, then glanced back at the newspaper lying alongside. The article—on the front page, no less—with the headline PRACTICALLY A VIRGIN, stood out in bold, block type just above Miranda's picture.

Talk about getting scooped.

His stomach turned as he realized how badly his good intentions had gone awry. Tossing the newspaper in his out box, Noah groaned. No one told him *The Bull Report* was going to run a special precontest exposé on the nominees. No one told him they'd use his nomination letter for quotes, or that Miranda's sister, Teri, would reveal the contents of Miranda's diary to the twenty thousand students who attended the Tampa campus.

Maybe she'll be flattered, having her personal life held up to her students as a prime example of smart choices and clean living. A reward for putting her career, her students and her family before her own personal needs.

Yeah, right.

Noah stuffed the letter in his shirt pocket beside the Snickers bar he'd intended to eat for breakfast and the cigar he was saving for after lunch. He didn't have much of a choice but to seek out Dr. Carpenter before her next class and do some serious explaining.

And some damage control.

He'd tell her the truth, of course. He'd seconded Miranda's nomination as the Most Virtuous Woman on Campus with a letter of recommendation and the best of intentions. He knew Miranda supported the C.I.S.S. group. Their goal to bring morality and virtue into the limelight of the new millennium was admirable—courageous even.

Besides, Miranda's sister, Teri, could be very convincing.

"I just want to show my sister what a role model she is to her students," Teri had argued. "Not like me. But we can't all be party animals like I am. Or you. Right?"

Party animal? Served him right to be saddled with such a ridiculous reputation. Fact was, after two failed relationships—one that involved a divorce decree and the other requiring several restraining orders—he *had* taken to hitting the nightlife rather hard. A different woman on his arm every night followed by quick goodbyes before anyone got the wrong impression. He'd been upfront and clear with each and every woman—he had no intention of seeing them again. No hurt feelings. No broken hearts. No boiled bunnies in his Crock-Pot—or in his case, no prized set of autographed baseballs served crisp and fresh from the fireplace.

After that experience, the only thing Noah Yeager committed to was a reputation as a man with no commitments. Even the elusive allure of fellow faculty member Miranda Carpenter hadn't deterred him. The fact that she showed no interest in him beyond friendship wasn't the point.

Noah ripped the wrapper off his candy bar and took a bite, then another. When his jaw ached from munching caramel, peanuts and nougat, he admitted to himself that he was a gullible fool in believing Teri Carpenter capable of goodwill. Though Miranda had used her considerable clout to place her younger sister as artist-in-residence, Teri reciprocated by spilling Miranda's secrets to a student reporter who obviously missed the class on ethics in journalism.

The world now knew that Miranda hadn't had a date since 1996—when she'd attended a family wedding with the bride's gay brother. The public could also read, in excruciating detail, about Miranda's awkward adolescence, her heartrending crush on her high-school biology teacher and her first and, from all accounts, last sexual encounter with a teenage boyfriend as adept in pleasuring a woman as Noah was in making a relationship last.

Crass as it was, the headline fit. PRACTICALLY A VIRGIN described Miranda's experiences to a T.

His gaze drifted back to the picture beside the article. At least the reporter had the decency to use a flattering photo, though Noah doubted the hack could have found a snapshot that didn't do the woman justice. Beauty like Miranda's didn't come from the nearest makeup counter, nor was such charisma glorified on television or in fashion magazines. Her features were too delicate, too ethereal, her lavender eyes too wide with unmatched intellect to be appreciated by the general public.

But in private... Noah's appreciation ran deeper than he'd ever admit.

Thankfully, she didn't share Noah's secret admiration. A single hint of desire on her part and he'd be lost for sure.

So why then did he want to use this situation to get closer to her? Show her his charm wasn't just an act? Prove he could be the man she'd obviously been waiting for?

Noah shoved the rest of the chocolate into his mouth, chasing the confection with a generous gulp of tepid coffee. In pursuit of learning more about Miranda than her professional credentials and her strange relationship with her sister, he'd helped sacrifice her privacy. He'd meant to show her that he admired more than just her academic talent. To unchain one of the fences she built around herself. To cultivate a real friendship.

But thanks to his poor judgment and Teri's loose lips, he'd now need a hacksaw and a locksmith to break through her defenses.

Miranda was a "retreater"—a personality type he'd coined shortly after working with her on a paper. They'd clashed on several key points, though he soon learned that Miranda preferred to step back from controversy and let the facts speak for themselves rather than take up the gauntlet in a war of words. While her tactics usually brought her victory, a less tutored observer than himself would have labeled her aloof. Dispassionate. Cold even.

He suspected none of those descriptions applied. Yet if he didn't act fast, he might never know for sure. And even worse, Miranda's critics at the university would have ample ammunition to box her forever into an unflattering stereotype.

He dialed her office, relieved when her voice mail listed her schedule for the day. He checked his watch. Her first class had started twenty minutes ago.

He tossed the Snickers wrapper in the garbage. Drawing on his extensive knowledge of psychology and his firsthand experience with angry women, Noah had a pretty good guess of how Miranda would react to the article and the nomination.

She wouldn't do anything, wouldn't say anything, no matter how much she seethed inside. Despite the hit her credibility would take—and Noah knew college students well enough to predict that Miranda would lose face in the classroom—she'd never defend her personal choices to anyone.

Considering his role in her humiliation, the least he could do was save her from herself. Force her to face this. Confront the conflict. And perhaps, in the process, he could find a little salvation of his own.

1

"WHAT DO YOU KNOW about sex anyway?"

Miranda had expected that question—loud and public and smack in the middle of her lecture on the hormonal effects of sexual arousal on the female brain. Just as she feared, this morning's front-page exposé in the student newspaper called to question the very essence of her credibility as a scientist and educator.

What she hadn't anticipated was the question coming from Dr. Noah Yeager.

She turned away from the white board and faced her class. The full auditorium of college undergraduates had politely failed to mention the article even though each of them carried a copy between their books. Unfortunately, Noah had never shown such a preference for diplomacy. He preferred charging straight ahead and "confronting the conflict," his favored phrase. Anything to avoid a snowball of emotion.

Now wasn't the time to tell him he was just a little too late.

PRACTICALLY A VIRGIN, the headline screamed, followed by a detailed account of Miranda's personal life—courtesy of her sister. After making countless references to Miranda as the "Mother Superior of the Church of No Fun," the reporter concluded, "Professor Carpenter lectures from her lab results. There's a difference between being virtuous and being ice-cold, but this reporter doubts Dr. Carpenter knows the distinction."

The byline identified a former student, one who'd failed Miranda's course on the Endocrinology of Sex and Reproduction. Sour grapes aside, the young journalist wrote nothing untrue. But that didn't mean Miranda wanted her secrets shared with the world. And while she knew her sister, Teri, deserved the brunt of her anger, Dr. Noah Yeager and his ill-timed intrusion weren't totally free from blame.

His quotes for the article had added just the ammunition the contemptuous reporter needed. Though Noah's original statements had been suspiciously reduced to one-word sound bites, his descriptors, like "sensible," "erudite" and "ethereal" adequately fueled the reporter's unflattering portrait.

And what did he mean by ethereal *anyway?*

What was she, some wispy, fragile, hothouse flower with little substance and not an ounce of grit? *Ha!*

She pushed her glasses up higher on her nose. "What do *I* know about sex? There's an answer you're not likely to find out, Dr. Yeager." She pressed the cap on her dry erase marker and stepped off the dais. "At least not firsthand."

A rumbling of "oohs" and reluctant laughter erupted from her students. Some shifted in their theater seats, folding back the tiny desktops and leaning forward expectantly. Others closed their notebooks and pocketed their pens, prepared to witness a battle. Too bad they'd be disappointed. Despite her tart retort, Miranda had no desire to air her grievances in public any more than she wanted the world to know that losing her virginity had *not* been a mind-shattering experience. Which, thanks to the article, everyone now knew.

"Is there something I can do for you, Dr. Yeager?" *Other than face this humiliation in a public forum?* "If you simply stopped by to apologize, I accept."

Noah stepped down into the auditorium, flipping a folded paper into the nearest trash can. Digging his hands into the pockets of khakis that looked like they hadn't seen an iron since he bought them, he glanced down at his sockless, dock-shoed feet before staring up beneath thick eyelashes to plead his case. "I do apologize for interrupting your class, but not for my part in your nomination. You are a remarkable woman, Dr. Carpenter. Incredible intelligence. Extraordinary compassion." The corner of his mouth twitched as he fought a smile. "An extraordinary capacity to forgive."

Miranda crossed her arms over her chest and groaned, though her exasperation soon turned to a reluctant grin. For a grown man obviously prepared to grovel, Noah Yeager walked with the confidence of someone well aware of his charm and completely prepared to use it. His tawny hair—windblown from his ride onto campus in the neon-blue toy he called a sports car—curved and curled around a high forehead, slightly stubbled cheeks and a block-square jaw. His skin caught a pinkish hue that told her he'd either just come in from a tennis match or he was more than a little uncomfortable with his current course of action—despite that bold confrontation was his preferred method of getting his way.

Miranda turned to her textbook and focused on the highlighted passage. If she noted the particular shade of his eyes this morning, gazed too deeply into his lethal baby blues, she might as well dismiss her class now. That one particular shade of turquoise, mixed with his irrepressible humor and innate intelligence, already had her more friendly with him than she had ever, ever planned to be.

Coupled with the fact that he was gorgeous as all get-out and a notorious heartbreaker, Miranda knew when she couldn't win. She wasn't afraid of a challenge and didn't shy from pushing herself academically, but she protected both her heart and her privacy with all the tenacity of a guard dog.

And Dr. Noah Yeager was like a thief in the night.

Luckily, Katie Brown, Miranda's militantly feminist student in the third row, broke the tense line before Miranda got hooked. "You're not going to buy that crap, are you, Dr. C.?"

Katie sneered as Noah passed, making her nose ring catch the fluorescent light.

"No, Katie, I'm not," Miranda said, mentally chiding herself for allowing a personal matter to interfere with her job. "However, if Dr. Yeager would like to rephrase his apology into something lighter on charm and more on fact, I'd be delighted to listen— *after* class is over."

Noah glanced at his watch. "My interruption is entirely necessary. Besides, what I said wasn't a load of crap, as Ms. Brown so crudely phrased it. It's the truth."

"Seems the truth isn't always as liberating as one would hope," Miranda quipped, though her point was lost in the hiss of the whispers and quiet discussions that ensued around the auditorium.

The double dose of Tylenol she'd taken with her coffee wore off, leaving tiny tentacles of pain to snake around the inside of her eyelids. When she received the letter from the C.I.S.S., she couldn't decide whether to be flattered or insulted. She couldn't deny the contest was for a good cause. And her sense of humor, dry though it was, had served her in more humiliating circumstances than a small campus group's attempt at disseminating information about abstinence to a decidedly reluctant audience. Just as she'd been about to accept the nomination as a good sport, her teaching assistant had burst in with an armful of newspapers, mumbling something about getting her hands on all the issues on campus, when one slipped, headline up, onto Miranda's desk.

There, in black and white, were her deepest, darkest secrets. And despite that she'd written countless articles for prestigious medical journals, published an award-winning textbook and entertained speaking requests from universities as far away as

Stockholm, Miranda Carpenter had been exposed as a fake when it came to knowledge about sex. She might be an expert on the physicality and physiology, but when it came to old-fashioned practical experience, she didn't have a clue.

She hadn't had time to figure out why her sister would betray her so thoughtlessly. They weren't exactly a textbook example of inseparable siblings, but they weren't Jan and Marsha Brady either. At least, not anymore. She thought they'd put their childish jealousies and petty pranks behind them.

Obviously, she was wrong. But she'd decided to waylay that line of thinking until after she was done with her class.

Right now, realizing that the entire population of the University of Southern Florida now knew about her sexual inexperience was bad enough. Knowing beyond a doubt that Noah Yeager also knew made her stomach hurt.

"Dr. Yeager, I really think we should postpone this discussion until class is over. These students have an exam next week and I'd like to make sure they're prepared."

"An exam on sex?" he asked.

"That is the general topic of this course."

His expression, incredulous as it was, bordered on laughable. Noah Yeager was a scientist of great respect and a beloved professor, but he couldn't act dumb worth a darn.

"But how can you be an expert on sex? You're..."

He grabbed the newspaper from Katie and made a show of skimming the article.

"Practically A Virgin." Miranda walked over and tapped the headline with her marker. "It's hard to miss."

"Aren't you embarrassed by that?"

Now she knew his game. Typical Noah. *Confront your conflict.* Psychologists! They rarely knew when to leave well enough alone.

Of course, "well enough" didn't exactly describe her this morning. She wasn't merely embarrassed— she was mortified. Never in her life had her credentials as a scientist been questioned on the basis of her personal life. Not only was she livid that her sister would mount such a sophomoric attack, she resented the paparazzi-like invasion of her solitary life-style. Stepping in front of her class after this morning's headline was the hardest thing she'd ever done.

She'd thought about retreating. Hiding. Turning her class over to her T.A. and locking herself away in her office until the attention died down. Instead, she'd forced herself to begin her lecture three minutes before the class's official start time, effectively avoiding any and all questions her students invariably had.

And Noah, being the man he was, wasn't about to let her get away with such roundabout cowardice.

"Of course," she admitted. "Who wouldn't be embarrassed by this article?"

"I don't know." He addressed the class. "Is there

anyone who read this article who doesn't think Dr. Carpenter should be embarrassed?"

Katie, of course, was the first to speak up. "Screw the reporter, Dr. C. Your sister Linda-Tripped you. She's the one who should be red-faced."

Miranda bestowed her pupil with the most patient expression she could muster. "I'm sure Teri meant well." *She'd better have meant well or I'm going to kill her.* "Reporters sometimes put a slant on things that the person being interviewed didn't necessarily mean."

Katie's pencil-thin eyebrows shot up at the same time as Noah's bushy ones.

"It's only fair to give her the benefit of the doubt," Miranda defended. "Besides, I thought bashing reporters was the national pastime."

"Baseball is the national pastime," Noah reminded her. "Apparently, coming in a close second is trashing your family in the media."

"The reporter has a point." Barely a whisper, the voice from the corner grabbed everyone's attention. The speaker, a burly football player who rarely contributed to class, shifted in what little space was left between his huge body and the tiny auditorium chair.

"What point? Go back to studying your play book, Bubba," Katie snapped. "Only a moron would see a point in that tabloid."

"Name's not Bubba, Femi-Nazi Chick-in-Black."

"Sorry, I thought all gridiron goons liked to be called Bubba," Katie returned.

"And I thought all menhating, nose-ring-wearing—"

Miranda held up her hand. "Hold on, both of you. Open dialogue will not degenerate into insults—not in *my* class. And since Dr. Yeager so *graciously* opened this up for debate, I think I'd like to hear what Mr...."

"O'Connell. Liam O'Connell."

"...what Mr. O'Connell has to say. Although, in exchange for your input on this topic, I'd like to see you chime in on actual course discussion next class, as well. Deal?"

Liam grinned sheepishly. "Yes, ma'am."

When he remained quiet, Miranda leaned back on her desk and let her arms drop to her sides. She really did want to hear his opinion, though she was nearly certain she already knew what it was.

"Go ahead, Liam."

His thick-fingered hands shook as he gripped the article. "You're always talking about using common sense to outwit chemical reactions. About thinking beyond our hormones."

"Yes, I am. It's not an easy task, but it can be done."

"But you haven't done it. Not really. You just...avoid the chemicals."

A clichéd argument sprang to mind. Without a more convincing rebuttal, Miranda gave it a shot. "One doesn't have to snort cocaine to know how dangerous it is. Or be an alcoholic to talk about the detrimental effects of binge drinking. You hear about that during this course as well."

Liam frowned. "This is different. I mean, when you're with someone you really, really like, you can be smart and not do anything to hurt anyone, or yourself. Condoms and birth control. But you preach abstinence."

Noah grabbed that moment to slip into an empty chair in the front row. Nearly a head taller than most of the coeds, he slid down low in the seat, stretching his lean, long legs to the center dais and crossing his ankles over the bottom step. Talking about abstinence in such close proximity to the sexiest man she'd ever met forced Miranda to draw on every professional bone in her body.

Still, she'd best keep this discussion short.

"Abstinence is the safest sex."

"No, it's *no* sex," Liam countered. "And that's an easy decision to make when you don't date. You don't know how tough it is. You don't know."

Miranda nodded, unable to respond. What could she say? Liam, in all his understated eloquence, was right.

She didn't know. She'd allowed herself one opportunity to experience the freedom of sensual discovery—and when that experiment failed miserably, she decided she'd gotten what she deserved for being so irresponsible. Better to concentrate on her studies and her career. She'd planned to waylay personal relationships only until after college, but watching her sister make mess after mess of her own life convinced Miranda that men weren't worth the trouble. They lied. They cheated. They could break a woman's spirit with no less than an unmade phone call and no more than an ill-chosen word.

So she taught abstinence and preached self-reliance. Even forged a reputation for herself as a mix between Dr. Laura and Dr. Ruth. So much so that a local radio network had called her literary agent to inquire about putting Miranda on the air. But until the details of that pipe dream were worked out, she had a classroom crowded with young minds ready, willing and able to challenge her authority and knowledge. How could she convince them, with her own mind overloading with doubt?

Abstinence? With men like Noah Yeager prowling the universe?

Impossible.

And yet, she'd found a way to resist Noah's powerful sex appeal over the past three years, though realistically, he'd resisted her right back—and seemingly, with much less effort.

"Liam, right?" Noah jumped in from his silent spot on the sidelines. Miranda almost stopped his interruption, then realized he owed her. He wasn't responsible for the article or her initial nomination, but he was completely at fault for making her face her turmoil in front of her students. The least he could do was cover for her until she came up with a reasonable counter for Liam's argument.

"Yes, sir, Dr. Yeager."

"Have you taken any psychology classes?"

"No, sir. Sex and Repro finishes my science credit."

A nervous twitter rippled through the room. The

title of her course alone resulted in her full classes and waiting list. When the department titled the course Reproductive Studies, barely ten people enrolled. Adding the word *sex* lured them in in droves.

"You should consider an elective then. I have a study I'm hoping to do soon—" he shot Miranda a hopeful look "—that will gauge the psychological effects of sexual relations, after the physical act. Sound interesting?"

Liam shrugged. "I guess. What does that have to do with Professor Carpenter?"

"You referred to the difficulty of combating those hormones when you're out with someone you have a strong attraction to. Dr. Carpenter is well aware of the long-lasting psychological effects of intimate involvement, so she's found an effective means to avoid it—until the right man comes along."

Miranda caught Noah's furtive glance. *Until the right man comes along?* He didn't mean him, did he?

"That's not realistic," Liam insisted, shaking his head and demanding Miranda's attention. "You don't find the right guy by locking yourself up in the library."

"Depends on what you're doing in the library," Katie added, eliciting chuckles from the entire back row.

"Okay," Miranda broke in, "I think this conversation has strayed far enough. I'm all for a 'teachable' moment, but I've had my fill of other people discussing my personal choices about my private life. Class dismissed."

A few students shot out of their chairs before Miranda changed her mind. The majority lingered, shocked that she'd let them out a single second before eleven o'clock.

"What about the contest?" Katie asked. "Isn't that all about your choices? Not that I'd blame you for pulling out."

Katie threw out the last comment with less candor than usual. Or at least, with less tenacity. She would "blame" Miranda for withdrawing from the contest, the action she had planned to take immediately after class. Her students, even the supportive ones like Katie—and in his own way, Liam—now had ample reason to question her authority on the subject of sex.

Thanks to the reporter, they now viewed her as nothing more than a mouthpiece for a textbook. She had no personal knowledge to draw on, no emotional investment in her subject. Her course was about to become dry facts and heartless lab results, no matter how much she loved her job.

And she certainly wouldn't make much of a difference that way. The contest would give her a forum to make her views, however conservative, much more clear. And since the competition involved a "public" date, she could also show her students that she was capable of enjoying interpersonal interaction without carelessly falling into bed.

"You won't pull out, will you, Miranda?"

Noah hadn't moved from his seat, and yet his deep-throated whisper, made painfully intimate by his use of her first name in a place where such familiarity was distinctly taboo, teased the edges of her hearing.

"I haven't decided," she answered, her voice uncontrollably quiet.

"I could help you decide," he offered.

Spoken in a devilish tone, his innocent words curled along the base of her neck.

Instantly, her inherent skepticism jumped to the rescue. "I'll just bet you could."

The remaining students quieted. Liam's dumbfounded expression mirrored the faces of nearly every student in the room. Had one professor just come on to another professor in front of God and everyone?

Miranda smiled ruefully. She knew exactly what Noah was up to, and breaking professional protocol wasn't his aim.

"What Dr. Yeager is proposing is that he provide the one element Liam seems to think is missing from my life—real temptation."

NOAH GRINNED, savoring his attempt to manipulate someone who was completely aware of his design. Unlike other women he'd sparred with, Miranda was his equal in all areas except one. If the newspaper article contained any truth at all, she was more emotionally dangerous than even Sarah, his Glenn-Close-in-*Fatal-Attraction* ex-girlfriend. While Sarah simply had a love-hate relationship with reality, Miranda believed in happily-ever-afters. Soul mates. Perhaps those walls she erected around herself shouldn't be earmarked for demolition. The rubble could end up crushing him.

He'd have to take that chance. Though he could definitely fall for her in a big way, his growing fascination with Miranda Carpenter had already skewed his better judgment. Unless he took a proactive stance and explored this attraction completely, but cautiously—he could find himself in more trouble than even a woman-scorned could cause.

"Temptation?" Noah stood, straightened his slacks and stepped forward, attempting to ignore the full auditorium of coeds behind him. "I've never been called that before."

"Ha!"

Miranda dropped her staid veneer with a single syllable, making Noah wonder how sturdy that facade was after all.

"If even an iota of your reputation is accurate," she said in a voice meant only for him, "I seriously doubt there isn't a name you *haven't* been called."

He nodded and frowned, yet again conceding her point.

"Not all of the names I've been called have been negative." He matched her whisper with his own, then raised his voice for the benefit of her students' straining ears. "Nonetheless, Professor, as the article stated, I seconded your nomination and, effectively, got you into this mess. The least I can do is help prove to your students that you can stick to your values, even when in the company of a guy like me."

"Like you?" She pushed her glasses back, ever so

slightly enlarging the size and shape of her incredibly lavender eyes. "What kind of guy is that?"

Katie ticked the words off like a practiced recitation. "Arrogant, womanizing, conceited, gullible..."

"Katie," Miranda chided.

"No, she's right—about the gullible part anyway. The nomination was never meant as a put down. The C.I.S.S. group really does admire you. And if we're looking for silver linings, the controversy over the interview will stir some interest in the cause."

Miranda watched as her students flipped the pages of the newspaper away from her article to the indepth coverage of Sexual Awareness Week. Thanks to Noah's invasion, and Liam's observation that undoubtedly reflected the thoughts of her other students, at least those that hadn't deserted, today's lecture was over for good.

Yet, as Noah said, interest had been stirred.

Glancing at her watch, she realized she'd only relinquished twenty minutes of the lecture. She dismissed the class once again, promising a more focused discussion on Wednesday.

"Hang tough, Dr. C.," Katie said as she pushed her books into the leather-and-studs knapsack that coordinated nicely with her similarly styled jeans and layered black-on-black tank tops. "That reporter probably just has the hots for you himself."

Miranda's skin crawled. "Katie, please. That does nothing to alleviate my horror."

Laughing, Katie bounded up the steps out of the

room to catch up with Liam, leaving Noah to slide back into a flip-down chair in the front row.

Miranda glanced around the deserted classroom. The space was cavernous, somewhat outdated and painfully impersonal. But private? Intimate? Miranda wouldn't have thought so until this very moment. The echoes of the retreating students disappeared with the soft click of the closing door. So did her sense of safety. Knowing no other class met here until after lunch, Miranda squashed the irrational panic that she and Noah would be discovered—here, alone—doing nothing more than carrying on a conversation.

She stacked her books together, deliberately turning her back on Noah. "If you're done forcing me to face my most humiliating moment, you're free to go. Forgive me if I don't thank you."

"Don't you feel a little better, getting it all out in the open?"

"I would have preferred to deal with this mess my own way."

"Which would have been to remain silent and let your reputation speak for itself."

Miranda slapped her file folders together and shoved them into her attaché, exasperated both by his insistence on invading her privacy and by the way she felt suddenly crowded in a very large, very empty room. "You don't think my reputation could have withstood that attack?"

He opened his mouth, then stopped to think. Miranda waited, her foot tapping.

"No. And neither do you."

"Thanks for the vote of confidence." Miranda heard her biting sarcasm and cringed. She liked Noah, she really did. She'd even let herself believe that they were friends—in the ways that colleagues can be. They spoke in the faculty lounge, shared research materials and even cowrote an article last semester—a feat accomplished almost entirely by e-mail even though their offices were only two floors apart. But always, Miranda remained at arm's length—no matter how hard she found it not to surrender to the fantasies Noah evoked with no more than a friendly "good morning." Like now.

From the moment the dean introduced them, Noah enkindled sparks of sexual awareness that even Miranda's extensive knowledge of pheromones and other hormonal influences could neither explain nor counteract.

But Miranda was no swooning coed. She knew better than to risk her heart on a man with Noah's reputation and devotion to a commitment-free life-style. While she was certain that sex with him would more than make up for the disappointment in her past, she wasn't about to become a notch on his bedpost. Self-respect and confidence led her to her successes. An affair with the likes of Noah Yeager could only bring heartache and despair—once the ecstasy wore off.

So long as she didn't become one of his conquests, how he conducted his personal life was none of her business. Their interactions were professionally friendly, and would remain so—as long as he stopped talking about *temptation.*

"So, are we on or what?" Noah sprang up from his seat with all the alacrity of a man who wouldn't hesitate at jumping over a net after winning a match.

"On? What are you talking about?"

"The date? I just happen to have this swanky event I have to go to this Friday night. It'll be perfect."

Her? Noah? In evening wear? Drinking wine and sharing small talk and generally learning more about each other? What if the reporter sensed the attraction she and Noah so carefully ignored? What if Noah's boundless charm enticed her to drop her guard— even for a moment—under the watchful eyes of the press?

She turned back to her briefcase.

"Noah, I don't think that's a good idea."

His groan was childlike. His hands, suddenly on her shoulders, were not. "Come on, Carpenter. This is perfect timing. I've applied for a grant with the Henson Foundation, and Mrs. Henson adores your work. She's announcing her decision on the Henson Grant at the reception Friday. You could be my ace in the hole. I need you."

The massage he gave her mimicked a coach's confidence-injecting rubdown, yet the warmth of his hands and strength of his fingers inspired images of bare flesh and hot oils. Miranda called on all her self-control to keep from overreacting and pulling away. Or worse—turning around and kissing him.

"Need me?" She forced steadiness into her voice.

"You could get a date in a roomful of nuns, Dr. Yeager."

"Ah, but would the good sisters be as intelligent as you? As entertaining as you? And the big question..." He dropped his palms down her arms, igniting the silk of her sleeve with a gentle friction. "Would they look as alluring in evening wear?"

She took the opportunity to slip her briefcase off the desk and step away. "Black seems to suit most of them. And you've never seen me in evening wear."

"I have. The alumni anniversary shindig last semester. Want me to tell you what you were wearing?"

No. She didn't even want to consider the possibility that he'd noted her apparel that closely, though from the lusty look in his eyes when she turned, he clearly recalled the fitted, beaded burgundy sheath her sister had convinced her to wear.

"I know what I was wearing, thanks." Miranda headed toward the steps, hoping to reach the sanctuary of her office before Noah changed her mind. She'd barely taken the second step when he snatched her briefcase and jogged ahead to open the door.

Chivalry? How was she going to combat chivalry?

"Consider this a chance to kill two birds with one stone," Noah reasoned. "Actually, three birds. You help me win my grant, I help you win your contest and at the same time, we learn a little more about each other."

She reached the doorway, thankful the hall bustled with students. None spared them even a glance, but she still felt safer with Noah in a crowd. "I'm not sure I'm going through with the contest. I don't enjoy the spotlight the way Teri does. And contrary to my sister's negative appraisal of my life, I like it the way it is. No pressure. No entanglements."

Noah grinned, teeth and all. Miranda sighed in surrender.

"No entanglements," Noah promised. "Just my style."

That was what scared her the most.

2

"IT'S ALL ABOUT DESIRE. Wanting. Needing. Right to the core of your being. You can't breathe. You can't see. Until the lust is fulfilled. Truly fulfilled."

Miranda shifted in her seat, grateful that the theater department had replaced the old, creaky folding chairs with soft, quiet benches before her sister became artist-in-residence. She'd slipped into Teri's workshop unseen, hoping to catch her as soon as the actors completed their rehearsal of a montage of scenes from Tennessee Williams. *It would be Tennessee Williams*, Miranda lamented. No staid, Victorian tea-time comedy for her sister. She specialized in producing and acting in plays that pushed the limits of propriety and social mores. Much to Miranda's chagrin, Teri's entire life pushed that limit—and was a certifiable mess as a result.

Just like hers was, since Teri had finally managed to inject her personal chaos into the order that was once Miranda's life.

"Some of you are just too young to have experienced an all-consuming passion," Teri lectured, finally catching sight of Miranda in the darkened corner. Her Cheshire-cat grin sent chills up Miranda's spine. "Not that age has anything to do with it, really. Take my sister, for example."

Miranda covered her eyes with her hands, pressing her fingers into her forehead, hoping to alleviate the pain. *No, this wasn't happening. Not again!* Did no one is this university understand the word *discretion?*

"You all read the article this morning. Here's a woman, just over thirty, sickeningly attractive..." Teri added a sneer that was only partly meant to invoke a laugh. "A virtual paragon in her chosen field, and she can't get a decent date."

Okay, Miranda decided. *Enough was enough.*

"Excuse me, Ms. Carpenter." Miranda held up her hand and stood, strengthening her aim to be recognized by the professor, with permission or not. "But let's stick to the facts. I can get a date. I *have* a date."

Teri's penciled eyebrows shot up beneath her jet-black bangs. "Really? That's news."

News? Miranda bit back a snide remark. "Weren't you just about to dismiss your class? It's after two o'clock."

Teri, who'd never worn a watch in her entire life, squinted to read the portable alarm clock she'd perched on a piece of errant scaffolding. "So it is. Go forth, thespians! Learn about lust and love if you can this week. You're going to need to if this production is going to work."

Miranda moved up to the front of the theater, eyeing each of the students pointedly. No one lingered, as was her intent. She was done airing her private life for public consumption—at least until Friday night.

After a substantial silence, broken only by the jingling of Teri's numerous bangle bracelets, Miranda climbed the steps onto the stage and slipped onto a stool near the dimmed footlights.

"What did I do?"

Teri continued to collect scripts from around the stage, pushing scenery and props out of her way. "What do you mean, 'What did I do?'"

"It must have been pretty horrible. Was it because I stole your Malibu Barbie when you were four and I was eight? I'm pretty certain I apologized for that. She didn't die in vain. My experiment on the burning point of plastic and rubber was the hit of the third-grade science fair."

"Miranda, what are you talking about?"

Miranda closed her eyes. If Teri knew what was good for her, before Miranda opened her eyes again, Teri's dumbfounded expression would be wiped from her pale pancaked face and russet lips and replaced with a repentant one.

"Think a minute, Teri." Miranda blinked open her eyes, but her sister's blank stare hadn't changed. "I'm talking about the same thing everyone else on campus is talking about. My pathetic attempts at romance? My status as an impostor in the arena of sexual knowledge? The damn article in *The Bull Report?*"

Teri threw her hands up and down as if washing away Miranda's concern. "Oh, that! Gosh, isn't it old news yet?"

Miranda took a deep breath and counted to ten. Her sister, who had always preferred the land of make-believe, sometimes had trouble grasping the nuances of reality. As always, Miranda took the responsibility of leading her back through the looking glass. Right now, she felt like shoving her through, but as always, she retained a tight hold on her impulses.

"It's not old news until it's old. Outdated. Join us here in the real world, Teri. We miss you."

Teri flipped up the houselights from a control at the edge of the stage. "Sarcasm doesn't become you, Miranda. Didn't Mother waste several bars of soap trying to show you that?"

"I'd take the sin of a smart mouth over the sin of betrayal anytime."

"I didn't betray you! Now who's being melodramatic?"

"I didn't call you *melodramatic.*" *Not today, anyway.* "What do you call it then when your sister reveals your most intimate secrets—to the press, no less?"

"Publicity?"

Miranda paused, hoping first that she hadn't heard right, and second that Teri would add something to her inane, one-word explanation to make her reasoning more clear.

She repeated her sister's word, making sure she'd heard her correctly. "Publicity?"

"Of course. Why else? I really didn't say everything the way it came out in the article, and I intend to give that young man a severe dressing-down when I see him, but you know what they say—bad publicity is better than no publicity at all."

Miranda slid off the stool. "Care to explain *why* I need publicity? I'm a professor, Teri. A scientist. Scientists don't need to be on the cover of the *National Enquirer*."

Teri rolled her eyes. "You can be so dense! Scientists probably don't need radio shows either."

Radio shows? Miranda's backside slapped the stool as the connections finally came into place—tenuously, but a pattern emerged. Last month, Miranda told Teri about the offer she'd received to host a syndicated call-in show discussing, of course, sex. She'd followed her story with a wayward comment to the effect of, "Who would want to listen to me?"

Had she inadvertently started the wheels of Teri's warped mind turning toward her humiliation?

"Let me get this straight. You wanted to drum up some interest in me as a personality so that I'd have a better chance at getting that syndicated show? And to do that, you revealed to my students my most private secrets?"

Teri's triumphant smile sent Miranda into a dizzying spin, even while sitting down. She pressed her elbows against her knees and cradled her head in her hands.

"Are you going to pass out? Do you need a pill?" Teri shot across the stage to the fringed bag she carried as a purse. "I have a pill. Give me a minute."

"I don't want a pill," Miranda said with a groan. *I love my sister. I love my sister.* The mantra did little to ease Miranda's migraine, but it did keep her from leaping onto her sister like an incensed Wonder

Woman, as she'd done plenty of times during their childhood.

Miranda was always the superhero. The defender. The paragon of virtue and righteousness. Teri preferred the role of evil villain, plotting maniacal schemes to take over the world, or at the least, steal freshly baked cookies from the metal racks where their mother cooled them. From all sides, their upbringing had been unusually traditional. Their father taught library science at Florida State, while their mother ran the household with love and precision. And yet, Miranda and Teri couldn't be any more different than if Teri had been the lost changeling of an alien race—a theory Miranda had never quite been able to prove to her sister, or her parents, despite her flowcharts and probability studies.

When Miranda looked up, Teri was sitting on the floor amid the spilled contents of her bag, watching her. And smiling. That devilish smile that meant Miranda was in for more trouble if she didn't clear out fast.

"What?" Miranda asked. "No. Never mind. Don't answer that."

"You look different."

"A migraine will do that to you."

"You don't get migraines. It's a stress headache. I'm done for the day. Let's go by the student union and I'll buy you a herbal tea."

"No thank you. The last place I want to be is in a crowded building filled with students who now know I've never had an orgasm."

Miranda flipped back her hair, patting the back of her head in search of the mate to the chopsticks that had, when she'd dressed this morning, held her hair in a loose twist.

"Want a pencil?"

"I want you to get me out of this mess!"

Teri shook her head. "No can do. Not my job. *You* get *me* out of messes, remember? And besides, you may be a little embarrassed, but you have a date! Tell, tell. With whom?"

Miranda smirked and pressed her lips together. She'd confided in her sister once before and look where that had gotten her. Luckily, she'd been smart enough to keep her errant sexual fantasies about Noah Yeager completely to herself. She didn't even write about him in her journal, a book her sister invariably found "by accident" whenever she came over for dinner. Unfortunately, Teri never once hid her attraction to the psychology professor with the hair that brushed passed his collar and the car with the removable top. She'd been making plays for Noah ever since she moved to Tampa from New York City.

"Never you mind. You can read about it in the Monday *Bull Report* just like everyone else."

"So you're going to go through with the contest? It really is a great idea." Teri shoved the contents of her purse back into place then slung the knitted strap over her shoulder. "I mean, I hear these kids talking about their sex lives. I'm the poster child for irresponsible behavior, but some of them make me look like...well, they make me look like you."

Miranda followed Teri off the stage and toward the exit. "Heaven forbid."

"Heaven gave up on me a long while ago, sis. I'm just glad you never have."

Bingo! And out of left field, too! Miranda winced as the guilt she shouldn't feel stabbed her smack in the gut. She'd prepared herself, prepped every righteous and indignant word she planned to unleash on her sister for her imprudence. Instead, Teri managed to find a way to make Miranda feel bad for getting angry.

"It's not going to work, Teri." Miranda stamped her foot for emphasis while Teri flipped off the light switches and turned the lock on the theater door. "I'm mad at you. Really mad."

Teri's smile was the ultimate example of condescension. "You'll get over it. Now, what are you going to wear Friday? Do you want to borrow something? I just bought this delicious butter-yellow, backless halter dress. In leather."

Miranda groaned as tendrils of anger slipped away. She was such a sucker when it came to her sister. "It's summer. No leather."

"You're worried about the heat? Trust me, there's not enough leather in this dress to make you sweat."

Sighing, Miranda followed her sister through the lobby while Teri described in detail the style of dress she had no intention of wearing, never mind the time of year. Even in the breeziest clothes, she wouldn't be able to escape the scorching temperatures Noah Yeager evoked with only his smile.

NOAH STOPPED, one foot over the threshold. With a hand on the doorjamb to keep him steady, he pushed back into the shadow of a tall bookcase overflowing with outdated newspapers and bound literary journals. This late at night and with a safe distance between now and final exams, the microfiche room at the library was usually deserted—which it was, essentially. Except for Miranda, and a student tending the desk way on the other side of the third floor, he hadn't seen anyone else since he jogged in to grab some reference materials for tomorrow's class on schizophrenia.

Dressed in a sleeveless sweatshirt and coordinating pants the soft, textured color of athletic gray, Miranda sat in front of a bulky microfiche scanner, her lavender eyes, pale cheeks and tawny hair reflecting the dim amber light. He'd caught her like this once before, alone in the stacks, engrossed in her work. He'd sneaked up behind her that time, jabbing her in the ribs and making her scream so loudly the desk attendant called campus security.

Tonight, he didn't feel so rambunctious. Now that he'd had his nefarious glimpse into her personal life, thanks to her sister and a reporter with an ax to grind, he found himself aware of her on more levels than he dreamed imaginable. The smell of her perfume not only beckoned him, but the very body of the fragrance—every crisp hint of ocean breeze, every subtle scent of citrus—reminded him that he'd read she adored the beach, an aspect of her he had never imagined. Even her hair color, a natural blend of blonds and browns kissed with a tinge of auburn, dared him to slip behind her and loosen the confining clips holding the strands sharply away from her face.

For the first time since this morning, when she'd tentatively agreed to honor their arrangement for Friday night, he wondered seriously if he was making a huge mistake. On the surface, Miranda seemed like a sweet, intelligent woman who just needed a little help loosening up. But he'd been wrong about women before. Best to tread lightly.

"Noah? Were you looking for me?"

He stepped fully into the room, chagrined that she'd caught him spying until he realized she obviously hadn't noticed his long stare. She'd already returned her attention to the microfiche, slipping the transparent card out of the viewer. From what he gathered, she'd already forgiven him for shanghaiing her class this morning. Not that he should feel relief. He had no doubt he'd soon give her another reason to be angry.

"I promised a student I'd find this article I'd read on the links between schizophrenia and prenatal cocaine use. What are you doing here so late? It's nearly midnight."

Miranda smiled ruefully and glanced at her watch. "I had some reading to catch up on. Sometimes I get restless at home or in my office. I like the library. The outdated equipment and musty smells have a certain charm, don't you think?"

Noah nodded, wondering how she could sense the odor of mildewing paper and decaying leather when all he could smell was her. All he could see was her. Even his hands, when he brushed by a stack of magazines waiting to be reshelved, itched to touch the suppleness of her skin. Before he could ask how the rest of her day went, she injected the silence with small talk.

"What about you? I thought you did all your research on the Internet."

He stopped across from where she'd swung her chair around to face him, her hands folded softly in her lap, her glasses slipped into the zippered neckline of her shirt. Her skin shimmered softly, as if she'd just worked out and the library's air-conditioning had cooled the sweat on her skin.

He licked his lips, wondering how salty she would taste if he kissed her right now. He couldn't—wouldn't—kiss her, but he couldn't help reaching out to stroke a wayward strand of hair from her cheek. "You shouldn't come here alone—at night. It's not safe."

For you or for me.

Her frown only intensified the plum pink of her mouth. With amazing subtlety, she leaned back in her chair, parting his touch from the soft plane of her blushing skin. "I'm a big girl, Noah. I can take care of myself. I've been doing it for a long, long time."

Standing, she slid her chair under the desk,

grabbed her bag, slipped a pencil behind her ear and scooped up a handful of note cards adorned with her illegible scribble—all without invading his personal space. "I have an article to find. I'll see you tomorrow."

She breezed by, leaving a gulf-scented trail in her wake. Noah had no choice but to follow.

"Miranda, wait."

He shook his head. One date—and an unconfirmed date at that—did not give him the right to go into Neanderthal mode. Just as he'd predicted, he'd wasted no time in pissing her off. But dammit, she didn't have to bolt. His comment had come from nothing more than a natural concern for her safety.

"Miranda?"

His voice echoed against the metal shelves that were spaced less than three feet apart and stacked with rows and rows of books. Without the sunlight from the wall of floor-length windows on either side of the building, the library's lighting was muted. Dim. Intimate. If he was a sane man or a man whose IQ accurately reflected his good sense, he'd turn tail and leave his research for another day. Unfortunately, he wouldn't do that.

He found her leaning against a bookshelf in a far corner, a book in hand, her tennis-shoed foot propped on a lower shelf just across from her. Sliding beside her into the cramped space, he stole a glance at the title of the article—"Virgins at Thirty."

She pressed the open book against her chest. "I

don't need a bodyguard, Noah. You can go about your business. Forget I'm here."

"I can't forget." He turned so his back pressed against the shelves opposite her and propped up his foot so they stood in identical stances, like images in a mirror. "Since this morning, I'm feeling responsible for you."

She slipped a note card between the pages to mark the article, then slid the heavy book onto an empty space on the shelf. "I'm not the psychologist here, but don't you think that's a natural reaction to the guilt you're feeling?" Crossing her arms over her chest, she resumed her relaxed stance, as if conducting a private conversation in a darkened, deserted library was something she did every day.

But Noah didn't. Images raced through his mind, the first a hazy fantasy of his fingers clutching the zipper on the front of her sweatshirt and pulling down. Slowly. Anticipating the shape and size and skin tone of her breasts beneath the soft cotton fleece. Did she wear a bra lined with lace? Perhaps the athletic type, with straight lines and a snug fit. Maybe, just maybe, she wore nothing at all.

"There could be a dozen causes," he answered.

"Like the fact that you need me to help you impress Amelia Henson on Friday night, and if I'm attacked in the deserted halls of the library, you'll be without a suitable date?"

"That's logical." But unlikely. More and more, Noah realized that the tight rein he held on his attraction to Miranda was quickly slipping away. If he didn't regain control soon, he'd find himself on the same dangerous path to heartbreak he'd been on before. First with Trish, his ex-wife, and then with Sarah. With each woman, he'd let his sexual attraction mute one undeniable fact—Noah couldn't commit. Even when he thought he'd fallen in love and made the trip down the aisle, he'd learned that he just didn't have the capacity to completely and honestly surrender that portion of himself that would make a union—marital or otherwise—complete and binding. And Miranda deserved more than that.

"I've been told logical is my forte," Miranda claimed, reaching across to match another book to a pencil-scribbled note card.

Noah stepped aside, allowing both of them some space. "Then it's only logical that I help you find what you need, so I can walk you to your car and you can get home safe and sound."

Flipping pages with her thumb, Miranda found the article and, marking it with another card, folded the book in her arms. She slapped her first find on top, then turned back to him with a smile.

"I'm done. What about you? Didn't you have something you wanted from the library?"

Wanted? Oh, yes. Miranda, naked, breasts round and ripe, her bottom pressed against the dusty books while he slipped inside and made her scream in ecstasy so loud the desk attendant called not only campus security, but the local police as well.

Not exactly a fantasy he could share with his wide-eyed colleague if he planned on her honoring their date Friday, an event he was looking forward to less and less as the minutes ticked by. They'd spent barely an hour together today and his mind brimmed with erotic reveries so vivid and so enticing, he wondered how he'd survive Friday night.

By using all your willpower, buddy. Every last ounce.

Gesturing toward the opening between the shelves, Noah stepped back so Miranda could pass. "What I need will have to wait."

3

HOT AND HEAVY, the steam from Miranda's shower clouded the bathroom with a fog so thick and humid, she threw open the door just to inhale. The haze immediately obscured the mirror in the dressing area of her bedroom, then dispersed with a rush from the air conditioner. If only ridding herself of wanting Noah was that easy.

She'd tried a cold shower first, but when the tingle of icy drops against her naked flesh conjured memories of Noah's cool touch, she added hot water. The soothing tinge of heat relaxed her muscles, but increased the intimate ache tightening her nipples. Would Noah's mouth surround her breasts with the same degree of heat? With the same wet warmth?

Attempting to burn the erotic reverie with a full blast of hot water hadn't helped either, so she'd bolted from the shower, dried herself quickly and escaped into her bedroom. At one o'clock in the morning, she should have been ready to fall asleep before she'd even pulled up her comforter or shut off the light. Her eyes were dry and heavy, her brain fuddled from exhaustion, her ability to reason derailed by the emotional roller coaster she'd ridden all day.

But climbing into bed would bring no relaxation.

Not with Noah's scent haunting her. Not when the gentleness of his touch or the nuances of his suggestive smile overwhelmed her conscious mind like a powerful hypnotic suggestion.

She didn't bother drying her hair, but instead combed it back and secured it from her face with a headband. Her class tomorrow started late; she'd restyle in the morning.

Throwing on a robe, she went downstairs and poured herself a glass of wine as she lit the scented candles Teri had given her last Christmas. Her library, a small room she'd hardly known what to do with when she first bought the house, bloomed with the flickering flames of dusty wicks. Soon, the space she'd decorated with thick carpets, fruitwood furniture and four walls of carved shelving, each brimming with her beloved collection of books, warmed with the scents of jasmine, vanilla and cloves.

She took another generous sip of full-bodied Cabernet, letting the intense, woodsy flavor touch every taste bud before she swallowed. Heat immediately infused her stomach, intensifying the heady dizziness she'd felt since her shower. After finishing a glassful, she refilled, took a longer draft, then slid her glass onto a marble-topped side table and used the dim candlelight to search for a book.

The glistening gold letters on *Lady Chatterly's Lover* caught her eye first. Then Wharton's *Summer* and Chopin's *The Awakening.* No matter how she tried, she couldn't escape. She imagined Noah as the hero in each of the stories she knew so well. Stories where women—prim and proper on the surface but boldly sensuous underneath—surrendered their souls to men of great passion, only to be destroyed by the very desires that gave them such ecstasy. Such freedom. Such tragedy. Miranda fingered the thin spine of Chopin's novella, picked up her wineglass and drank until the fermented grapes made her drowsy.

She recalled those tense moments in the library earlier that evening when she'd stood with Noah, alone, in the dusky solitude of the stacks, speaking in practiced whispers. Standing so near, the natural heat from his body caused trickles of perspiration to wind from between her breasts to the slope of her tummy. Just a moment of courage and she would have taken the half step she needed to stand chest to chest with him, her mouth level with him, her eyes gazing up into circles of blue.

Would he have touched her? How? Miranda turned her back to the bookshelf and clutched the wine to her chest. The glass pressed against the naked V where her robe split, to the spot Noah's gaze had explored, however briefly, in the confines of the university library. Draining the rest of the wine from the goblet, she imagined Noah's lithe fingers grasping the tiny silver clasp on her sweatshirt's zippered front.

If he'd pulled the zipper down in the library, he would have found a snug sport bra in cotton black. But if he slipped into her private library now and untied the sash on her robe, he'd reveal her, full and primed and naked. Miranda's lids pressed down over her eyes, blocking out the flickering candlelight, blocking out the last vestiges of reality surrounding her.

In this fantasy, she wasn't home. She was in the campus library, risking her career and her heart for an erotic interlude with Noah, a man who ignited fires deep inside her like lightning strikes in a dry, open field. Except Miranda wasn't dry. Moisture surrounded her, from the dripping strands of her hair to the wine-infused confines of her mouth to the juncture between her thighs. As her hand slid down between the fluffy sides of her robe, she shuddered. Noah *would* touch her like this. Slow. Skilled. Deliberately skimming the lower arc of her breasts until she cooed, then flicking upward to tease her tight nipples. Would he pinch them? Rub them between forefinger and thumb?

The room spun. Or was it her? Miranda could no longer be sure. The intoxicating mix of wine and wanton need sent her reeling. Grabbing the bookshelf, she steadied herself, her chin pressed against the carved wood. What was she doing? What was she thinking?

Rational thought didn't—couldn't—take root. Images and illusions of Noah pressed against her back, his erection thick and rigid between the curves of her bottom, kept reality at bay. Her body temperature soared. She pushed off her robe. She'd always wanted this. Always. With Noah. No one else. His hands surrounding her—one attending her breasts, the other between her legs, pumping a gentle friction that turned the darkness behind her eyelids into a living band of color.

Pleasure rocked her to the precipice. Erotic delight urged her to the edge. A stroke later and her legs weakened. Her breath deserted her. A sweet convulsion, an intimate quiver, and she found herself on the floor, her robe catching her like a soft cloud.

First, she blamed her fatigue. Then the nomination. Then the quiet library, her too-hot shower, the wine and her own untested libido. None of the recriminations took hold as she leaned sideways onto an overstuffed footstool and pressed her cheek against the cushion. Only just before she surrendered to sleep, she acknowledged the irony.

Noah had just given her her first orgasm—and he'd never even know it.

CHECKING HIS WATCH one last time, Noah tugged the sleeve of his tuxedo and decided to wait a few more minutes. He didn't want to seem anxious. He'd told Miranda he'd pick her up at seven o'clock. Showing up at six forty-five would make him look like a sap at best and an idiot at worst. And he was determined to be neither, no matter what his subconscious mind told him.

His degrees in psychology and his extensive knowledge of dream interpretation amounted to overkill when it came to figuring out the message behind his fantasies over the past few nights. As his date with Miranda approached, the images became more intense, more erotic, and more impossible to ignore. He felt like a prepubescent teenager.

The fact that unnerved him most was knowing Miranda wasn't attracted to him at all.

The sexual tension crackling between them in the library three nights ago had been undeniably one-sided. While he had exhausted all his self-control to keep from ravishing her in the dark, intimate setting of the very public campus building, Miranda had spoken with cool precision. Her eyes had met his boldly—without fear or desire or confusion—three emotions that even after nearly a week, assailed him every time he considered how he'd behave this evening. He'd vowed to keep out of any relationship that might cause a romantic entanglement. Judging by Miranda's indifference, he didn't have much to worry about with her. His own irrational passion aside, their friendship would remain as it always had: cordial, reliable, passionless.

And damn if that didn't annoy him to hell.

He turned off the ignition of his car and exited, clicking on the alarm just as a slick, ebony stretch limousine pulled up behind him outside Miranda's Mediterranean-style home.

Katie Brown popped out of the automatic sunroof dressed in an interesting combination of magenta taffeta ruffles and lacy black gloves, fingers removed.

"Hey, Dr. Y. Cool wheels, huh?"

Noah shoved his hands into the pockets of his pants. "Cool in an ostentatious, overdone sort of way. What are you doing here, Katie?"

Adjusting the angle of her tiara-like headband, Katie beamed before lifting a small camera from around her neck and snapping his picture. "Didn't Professor Carpenter tell you? I'm a journalism major this week, so she talked the campus newspaper into hiring me as a freelance reporter for the article on your date. After their screwup printing that libelous piece of trash on Monday, they didn't have much of a choice."

The driver slid out of the front seat and opened the door to the back, prompting Katie to pop down and emerge, black combat boots first.

"I must have missed the press release," he muttered.

She shrugged, undampened by his scowl. "Then I must be a most pleasant surprise."

He eyed her skeptically. "I'm reserving judgment until the end of the evening. Where'd you get the ride?"

"Courtesy of *The Bull Report.* I think the editor is nervous about a potential libel suit. There's even champagne! I don't suppose you'd forget, just for tonight, that I'm not twenty-one?"

Noah shook his head at Katie's pout, then turned to cross the small bridge that led over a decorative pond to the glossy stones in front of Miranda's door. He stopped when Katie's boots clomped close behind.

"Excuse me, Ms. Brown, but I'd like to greet my date in the traditional manner. That doesn't include a chaperon."

"Depends on your definition of traditional," she replied.

Noah swallowed a grin. "New millennium traditional, thank you. Look, Katie, I appreciate what you're doing. I think. But notwithstanding the thousands of research dollars riding on tonight, I want to make sure Miranda has a nice evening."

"You should. You got her into this."

He took a deep breath and slowly pulled his hands from his pockets and forced them to his side. *She's a kid,* he reminded himself. The fact that she harbored inordinately negative feelings toward men at such a tender age was her problem, not his. He *taught* psychology. And for tonight, he didn't *practice* it.

"Already been there, Katie. Dr. Carpenter and I have made our peace. I don't need you stirring up trouble. If that's what you plan, we'll take my car to the reception and give you little more than 'no comments' to weave into an article. Clear?"

Katie smirked, but nodded. She retreated into the limousine with a stamp of her boot, causing a flat imprint on Miranda's lush, meticulously landscaped lawn.

If he had any illusions about the night transforming into a romantic interlude, Katie Brown's presence shot that all to hell. Probably just as well, he mused, leaping over the two steps to the double front doors.

The doorbell chimed both inside and out, a flamenco tune that caught him off guard. He stepped back, perused the house from the Spanish-tiled roof to the expert gardening, then back to the address on the mailbox. Since the limo had arrived here as well, he must be at the right place, though he wasn't sure the house reflected the owner.

An air of Mediterranean romance, mingled with the scent of fresh blooming roses, conjured images of men in black masks, swooning *señoritas* and clashing, silver swords. The atmosphere tapped into fantasies he hadn't entertained since his father let him stay up late to watch reruns of old Errol Flynn movies.

Questions like *how* and *why* the steadily scientific and endlessly practical Miranda had chosen such a home disappeared when she opened the door.

He smiled, waiting for her to say "Hello" or "You're early" or, a long shot, "Could you zip this up for me?" She said nothing. Instead, she stepped back and whistled. An impressive wolf whistle, if ever he heard one.

He couldn't resist the urge to straighten his lapels.

"Hello, I'm here to see Dr. Miranda Carpenter, the noted scientist and world-renowned good girl."

Miranda clucked her tongue and licked her lips. Lips painted an alluring shade of brick red. "You know, if men were *really* smart, they'd use all that power they've amassed to change the world so they could wear tuxedos every day of the week."

Noah glanced sideways into the mirrored wall of Miranda's foyer. Was he imagining things, or did she just make him blush?

"A compliment? Well delivered. You're very good."

She shrugged, inviting him in with a wave of her

hand. "Admittedly, I don't get much practice. But Teri came over to help me pick out my dress. She coached me. Didn't think I could pull off the whistle. I guess I was properly inspired."

If he wasn't sure he'd look like an idiot, Noah would have knocked himself in the head to jog his sense. Despite his own carnal musings, this was the Miranda he knew. Cool and composed and, every so often, unpredictable. But still good as gold.

"I'll remember to thank Teri when I see her. That dress is...amazing."

Miranda, fiddling with the back of her earring in the foyer mirror, smiled at him through her reflection. "It should be. I could fund your research project myself with what I paid."

Every penny well spent, Noah concluded, his gaze following the lines of the dress—a lacy black sheath over a formfitting, flesh-colored slip—as they hugged Miranda's lithe curves. Delicate straps of satin draped over tanned shoulders. The neckline, though modest, molded to her breasts like his hands ached to—and provided just enough of a peek at her cleavage to heat the saliva pooling in his mouth.

"You look stunning. Thanks, Miranda," he said, somewhat surprised by the genuine gratitude lilting his voice.

"Thanks for what? For the dress?"

The dress alone did deserve great expressions of appreciation, but Noah knew women well enough to impart those in several well-timed, sincere compliments throughout the evening. He was thanking her for something much more personal.

"For accepting my invitation, despite my collusion with your sister in the Most Virtuous Woman on Campus contest."

Miranda grabbed her purse from a marble-topped, heavy oak table in the foyer and slipped a lacy wrap around her shoulders.

"Against my better judgment, I forgave Teri. Which is no great surprise since I've been forgiving her against my better judgment since she was two and threw up in my Sigmund the Seamonster lunch box."

Noah chuckled, distinctly remembering owning one of those himself.

"I forgive you, too," she admitted, her voice a whisper. She'd stepped closer to straighten his tie, though he was quite certain it wasn't crooked. "But you did promise me a good time tonight. I expect you to pay up. That means intelligent conversation, delicious food, a decadent dessert and at least one glass of champagne. Think you can handle that?"

She spoke in that matter-of-fact, don't-you-dare-contradict-me tone that earned her the respect of her students, but Noah couldn't help envisioning a decadent dessert that didn't involve chocolate or any other confection served after a meal. His gaze darted up the winding, wrought-iron staircase to her second floor. What he'd love to whip up was best served in a bedroom. Thinking twice, he realized chocolate could come in handy.

"Noah?"

Clearing his throat, he extended his arm and tugged open the front door, anxious to get on with the evening before he did something really, really stupid.

"Your wish is my command," he murmured.

Miranda snorted, inspiring laughter from Noah that warmed her insides like hot caramel fudge. Sweet and gooey and...comforting. Dangerously so. Miranda was intelligent enough to know a checkmate move when she saw one, but she was powerless to keep herself from sliding right into harm's way. Noah wasn't the kind of man who'd be interested in her for long. Sure, he wasn't intimidated by her academic achievements like so many of the men she knew. He didn't even seem to mind when she lost herself in her work and forgot to go home, or that she tended to take a moralistic high road in all situations, even if it wasn't politically correct.

The fact remained that Noah Yeager wasn't a marrying man—and before Miranda risked her heart, she was going to make damn sure she had a gold ring around her finger.

Miranda waved at Katie, who'd popped out of the top of the limousine like a tiara-topped rhododendron. She'd really have to talk to her newly acquired protégé about her choice in formal wear, then squelched that thought when she remembered that Katie was putting herself through college and usually made do with hand-me-downs from her older sister or treasures from the thrift store. She hadn't had the free rein of generous scholarships to finance her education as Miranda had. She also hadn't had the unconditional love of two parents. Katie's single mother did her best, but Miranda recognized the young woman's unabashed resentment toward men for what it was—anger at the father who abandoned her. She'd love to discuss the matter with Noah, to glean psychological insight on how to encourage Katie to heal, but she wouldn't have a chance tonight—thanks to her own devious mind.

After waking up late Tuesday morning and nearly missing her ten o'clock class because of a raging hangover, she vowed to take Noah's long-standing advice and make a defensive strike as soon as possible. Total exhaustion from grappling with more erotic dreams than she'd thought one woman was capable of having in a single night's time made thought difficult, but not impossible. Her first concern, even before she dealt with the student newspaper and their lame attempt at journalism, was figuring out a way to keep herself from succumbing to Noah's charm during their Friday-night date.

She'd swallowed three cups of extra-strong coffee and jotted down several useless strategies when Katie stopped by her office for career advice. After destroying the lists in the paper shredder, Miranda chatted with her student, soon realizing that Katie's inclination for stirring up trouble made her a natural for investigative journalism.

Just as quickly as Katie agreed, Miranda saw a way to solve two of her own problems at the same time.

First, she'd strongly urge the campus newspaper to hire Katie for the upcoming article on her date, no longer trusting the regular staff of *The Bull Report* to give her fair consideration. Second, she'd have a chaperon for the evening with a vested interest in keeping Miranda and Noah at arm's length. For tonight, Katie's men issues would work to Miranda's advantage. Starting first thing Monday, she'd see to it that Katie received sincere guidance in freeing her of her burden.

"Dr. C., you look hot," Katie gushed, wasting no time in snapping pictures despite the harsh sunlight.

Miranda slipped her sunglasses from her purse. "I'm squinting. Don't take pictures when I'm squinting."

Katie lowered the camera and pursed her lips with comic exaggeration. "Geesh. One date with Dr. Yummy and you're already vain? I think I have my headline."

Smirking, Miranda stepped aside so the driver could open the door. "You also have a grade to earn in my class. Don't think I didn't set this whole thing up with that in mind."

"A 'good girl' who blackmails," Katie assessed with a sigh. "This is going to be an interesting article."

Miranda slid into the seat, glad she felt such a comfortable rapport with Katie and wishing she had the same with Noah. When he climbed in beside her, his silky pant leg brushing against the lacy slit on the side of her dress, she forced herself to remember that she had shared a comfortable accord with him, until this whole date business.

"So," Katie broke the silence while the driver slammed his door shut and started a slow crawl down Miranda's driveway, "let's get started, shall we?" She pulled a small tape recorder from her sequined purse and pressed the record button. "Dr. Yeager, why did you ask Dr. Carpenter out on this date? You have a reputation for dating younger women—coeds even. No offense, Dr. C."

Miranda shook her head. "None taken. But don't make that crack again when I'm forty. I might not be able to handle it then."

The subsequent laughter broke the tension, but didn't distract Katie from her question. "I guess taking a former or present student to an important academic reception wouldn't do much to help you get your research grant, would it?"

Miranda felt Noah shift in his seat, an uncomfortable squirm that shimmied up her spine. "Katie, don't you think you should be asking *me* the questions? I *am* the subject of your article, not Dr. Yeager."

"I'm just trying to establish his reason for asking you out. It's my understanding that you've worked together for three years, but you've never had a date until now."

She'd done her research. Miranda knew Katie's innate affinity for investigative journalism could be both a blessing and a curse, but she didn't expect to feel the ill effects so soon.

"We prefer to keep our relationship professional," Noah answered.

Katie clicked off her recorder. "Well, if that's how this is going to go, then I might as well have you drop me off at the next corner. This is supposed to be a *real* date. You know, idiotic small talk, subtle flirting, uncomfortable silences followed by unexpected groping and a slap." Katie stopped for a moment to think. "Or not."

"Not all dates go the same way," Miranda reminded her.

"Not all men are the same," Noah added, his voice more pointed than Miranda expected. "Let's try an experiment, Ms. Brown. Save the interview for Monday morning. You have the facts. Why not make this an evening of observation?"

"Observation?" Katie asked.

Miranda's heart stopped when Noah wrapped his hand around hers and drew her fingers to his lips. Gently, his gaze fixed into hers, he placed a whisper-soft kiss on her flattened knuckles—once, then twice, until her breath caught audibly.

His blue irises danced with a mixture of naughty intentions and serious design. "Watch and learn, Katie." He kissed Miranda's hand once more, then smoothed her fingers beneath his chin before releasing her from his tentative grasp. "Watch and learn."

4

AMELIA HENSON KNEW how to throw a party. From the frosted tea lights woven into the evergreen shrubbery to the satin ribbons braided around the polished mahogany stairwell, the Henson estate shimmered with understated gaiety. Even Noah, a virtual stranger to the life-styles of the rich and famous, appreciated the simple good taste around him—when he could manage to tear his attention away from Miranda long enough to notice.

Luckily, his challenge to Katie to "watch and learn" diffused the cub reporter's interest in his past relationships and reputation. The rest of the car ride, she'd asked about Miranda's upbringing, leaving Noah to sit back, listen and do some learning himself. His childhood mirrored hers on several levels. A parent in higher education. One younger sibling. Traditional values strictly adhered to.

And yet, they couldn't be more different.

Upon their arrival at Henson House, Katie begged Miranda to accompany her to the ladies' room, leaving Noah to dwell on how two adults of similar backgrounds could end up so dissimilar. Genetics, he supposed. More than likely, gender played a strong role. But then, comparing himself to Miranda's sister didn't produce the same results. He and Teri were practically two peas in a pod, and yet, he had no interest in her whatsoever.

A crying shame, too. She was everything he should want in a woman. Attractive. Vivacious. Committed to no commitments.

But Noah wanted Miranda, the one who believed in gold bands and sacred vows and happily-ever-after. The one who'd never experienced good, thorough loving—a challenge in itself if he'd ever heard one. That challenge had invaded his dreams with erotic images and sensual delights all week.

Unfortunately, he was supposed to help Miranda *win* the Most Virtuous Woman on Campus contest. Lord knew, he was the one who needed help. Here he was fantasizing about stripping her bare when he'd promised to do everything in his power to keep her honest. Thankfully, they'd be spending the evening with Amelia Henson. With the power of age and wisdom at her command, this grand dame and her influence over his future would undoubtedly keep him on the straight and narrow.

Born an heiress to a family of phosphate magnates, Amelia Henson had earned a second fortune in her own right by inventing a "revolutionary" brand of condoms. One of the most reliable on the market, her prophylactics focused on enhancing a woman's pleasure long before anyone had discovered the G-spot, much less talked about it in public.

As had been her practice for the past thirty-five years, she'd set silver bowls of foil squares atop linen-covered sideboards in the foyer and in the center of several tables throughout the formal living room where everyone gathered. A proponent of safe sex long before the term became politically correct, the eighty-plus philanthropist now invested heavily in research and sex education programs, particularly for preteen and teenage girls. Noah's study on the psychological aftermath of intimate behavior, primarily on young women, was a perfect fit. Now he only had to convince his potential benefactor.

But keeping his eyes on the prize wasn't going to be easy. Despite his do-or-die mission and the presence of a hungry-for-controversy reporter, Noah could think of nothing more than finding a close, dark corner in Amelia Henson's sprawling mansion on Tampa's south side. Perhaps beneath a stairwell. A hidden room. Damn, he'd settle for a broom closet if he could just get Miranda alone. Perhaps with some wine.

Oh, yeah. And the chocolate.

He shook the notion right out of his head. Never a man of inaction, he'd resolved on a whim to show Katie Brown—and Miranda Carpenter—that he could be irresistibly charming, attentive and well-behaved when he wanted to be. He felt somewhat like a role model for the entire male population. While he highly suspected he was simply rationalizing a reason to pull out the stops with Miranda, Noah held fast to the belief that he could handle tonight without getting too involved.

So long as they didn't serve anything chocolate.

"Some digs," Katie breathed as she and Miranda rejoined him in the foyer. A gloved butler led them to a drawing room that looked exactly like a scene from *A Room with a View*. Uniformed servants spun through the crowd, balancing trays of gleaming crystal and champagne. Noah snatched two flutes, handing one to Miranda before ordering a ginger ale for Katie.

"Spoilsport," Katie grumbled. She snapped a few pictures of a genuine Tiffany lamp sitting beside a Fabergé egg. "This woman must be loaded."

"The Amelia Henson Foundation funds several studies each year, as well as four charitable institutions devoted to unwed mothers and abused children," Miranda said, impressing Noah once again with her knowledge. "You should try and interview her, separately from our article, of course. She endowed a chair in the psychology department over twenty-five years ago. I think her son was in the first class to graduate from USF."

Katie nodded, listening intently as she absorbed the information and the atmosphere around her. Obviously intrigued, Katie released her tractor-beam connection to Miranda and wandered off on her own. Noah was impressed.

"You're a good influence on her."

Miranda frowned. "Thanks. I think. I'm not sure I'm all that thrilled with being a good influence on anybody."

"Too much pressure?"

"You could say that." Miranda took a sip of her

champagne and glanced around the room, making it painfully clear she'd rather look at rows and rows of leather-bound books than at him.

"You don't have to be a good influence on me," he said.

She took a longer sip. "Why? Are you beyond my influence?"

His chuckle caused him to choke on his champagne.

"One of these days," he said, "we're going to have to sit down and discuss my reputation. Not everything that's said about me is true."

"You don't exactly do anything to make me, or anyone else, for that matter, think otherwise."

He nodded. "True. Sometimes a bad reputation comes in handy."

"*That* I wouldn't know."

Miranda spotted an acquaintance and, with a glowing grin, strolled away to greet her. Noah could swear he'd detected in her voice regret tinted with a light stroke of envious green. Did she covet the freedom his bad reputation gave him? He had to admit that he never had to worry about letting people down. Even his parents and sister, who seemingly knew him best, assumed the worst from him when it came to women. He'd never really thought about how much easier that made things until he caught the subtle melancholy in Miranda's voice.

Noah followed her, certain he'd heard her wrong. In the three years he'd known her, Miranda never contradicted the convictions she taught in her classroom—sparking the admiration he had for her from the beginning. Yet, thinking she might not want to be so singularly good all the time didn't lessen his respect for her one bit.

But it sure would make keeping his hands to himself a hell of a lot harder.

They spanned the room together, finally finding Amelia Henson sitting on a tapestry-covered window seat and holding court with Katie Brown and her tape recorder. This cub reporter obviously didn't waste any time.

"Dr. Yeager!" Amelia Henson extended her hand with the graceful ease of born-into-the-job royalty. "Ms. Brown here has been telling me all about your date with Dr. Carpenter. It's so good to finally meet you, dear." She took Miranda's hands warmly into hers. "I read your series of articles in the *New England Journal of Medicine*. Your conclusions about those studies on hormone treatments for menopause were brilliant, but your insights were especially poignant—like you'd been through it yourself."

"Thank you, Mrs. Henson. I seem to have a talent for understanding things I've never been through."

"Well, there's a time and a place for everything and everyone," she said sagely, causing Noah to wonder just how much Katie had told her about Miranda. "And believe me, firsthand experience sometimes isn't all it's cracked up to be."

She waved her hand and in a matter of seconds, a butler appeared with two straight-backed chairs.

"Join us. I'm terribly interested in hearing about

this contest you're involved in. 'The Most Virtuous Woman on Campus,' eh? A dubious honor in this day and age."

Miranda nearly choked on her wine, but recovered after placing the empty flute on a passing tray and sitting down. "I'm afraid you're correct about that. I wouldn't mind, really, if not for the toll it's taken on my credibility as a scientist."

Noah shook his head, marveling at Miranda's candor. Of course, women like Amelia Henson insisted on no less than the full and honest truth. And since Miranda didn't seem to know how to form a fib, much less an out-and-out lie, the women were a perfect match.

"Really?" Mrs. Henson asked. "How so?"

Briefly, and with several successful attempts at humor, Miranda related her experiences during Monday's class, including Noah's part in the entire fiasco.

"Well, Dr. Yeager, you must find yourself in a terrible quandary," Amelia concluded, sliding a caviar canapé onto a linen napkin from a waiter's tray.

Noah swallowed the salmon puff he'd just popped into his mouth. "A quandary? No. I mean, I'm honored to be Dr. Carpenter's date this evening. It'll give me a chance to show young ladies, like Ms. Brown here, that men do admire virtuous women."

Amelia barely managed to cover her mouth before an explosive guffaw shot her half-chewed hors d'oeuvre sailing across the room. "Oh, excuse me. But really, Dr. Yeager, don't play me for a fool. Or any of these women. Men may admire virtue, but they've started wars for the express purpose of conquering it. Hell, if men admired virtue even a quarter more than they do, my life's work would be saving stray cats instead of pregnant adolescents."

Noah smiled and nodded. What could he say? Arguing with the woman who held his academic future in her hands wasn't the most intelligent response. Besides, she was right.

"Well, Mrs. Henson, Dr. Yeager is a rare specimen among the males I've met," Miranda defended.

"Rare? Hmm. I've heard more than a few negative insinuations about his personal life—from some of the other applicants for my grant, of course, so I've taken it all with a grain of salt. Care to clarify anything?"

How the conversation shot from Miranda's reputation to his reminded Noah of the spinning, whirring sensation Wile E. Coyote must have felt whenever the Road Runner sped by.

"I don't believe my personal life has any more bearing on my credibility as a scientist than Miranda's."

He replayed his response in his head as he watched Amelia Henson mull over his words.

"I'm not sure I agree with that, but I'm willing to give you the benefit of the doubt. I've read the outline of your proposed study. Your theories, if proven, could do well in providing scientific support for legislation I'm lobbying for—a complete restructuring of sex education curriculum in the lower grades."

"Then you're leaning toward my study for your

grant?" Noah asked hopefully, knowing Mrs. Henson planned to announce her decision tonight, though he'd heard she hadn't yet made up her mind.

"Your competition is impressive, but I think your work could potentially do more good than the others. I'm not interested in pouring out thousands of dollars just to get a write-up in some obscure psych journal. I'm not going to be around forever and if I want to make a real difference in the lives of young people, your study may be the place to start."

Noah couldn't contain a proud grin, especially when Miranda squeezed his hand in support.

"We'll make a difference together, Mrs. Henson," he said. "I'm sure of that."

Amelia Henson's sage pink lips curved in approval. "Yes, yes. Well, now that that business is over, you have another theory to prove tonight. This young lady—" she gestured to Miranda with her wineglass "—needs to have a good time. My advice is lay off the finger food, enjoy the band on the south terrace, skip the first two courses of dinner and hold out for the desserts." She smiled nostalgically. "My husband, Marcus, used to arrange the most delightful romantic interludes when we were courting. The devil always served dessert first."

Katie, who'd remained silently intrigued throughout the exchange, looked almost wistful. "You gotta love a man who serves dessert first. All the guys I know would worry about what the calories would do to me."

"Then all the *guys*," Mrs. Henson pronounced the

word with a foreign discomfort "—you've dated weren't worth your time."

"You listen to Mrs. Henson, Katie," Noah instructed, standing and taking Miranda's hand.

"Where are you two going?" Katie asked.

Noah grinned. "To find dessert."

MIRANDA CARPENTER HAD BEEN many things in her lifetime, but speechless was rarely one of them. Still, she hadn't managed to string more than three words together since Noah had swept her away from Mrs. Henson. First, he'd snatched two flutes of champagnes from a waiter, then absconded with a full chilled bottle of Dom Perignon when the wine steward turned his back. After they raided the dessert cart of several decadent Black Forest petit fours, he swept her onto the south terrace and showed her how to dance the waltz.

Two other couples shared the marble dance floor, but the terrace spanned the entire southern side of the antebellum home, leaving them plenty of space to fumble and laugh as a six-piece band filled the night air with melodious strains of bygone days. Miranda had never danced like this before. After watching him box out the movements, then stepping on his toes twice and tripping over her own shoes once, the champagne finally took hold, allowing her to relax long enough to catch the natural rhythms flowing through Noah's body. Music was in his blood. And not just the rock and roll he blared from his car stereo or the CD-ROM on his office computer. Classics. Complex rhythms created to entice the soul.

And boy, was Miranda's soul enticed right about now.

She waylaid her interest with chitchat. "Where did you learn to dance like this?"

Noah inched closer; his hand slipped lower. Though it was still firmly on the small of her back, Miranda swore she sensed the heat of his fingers as they teased the uppermost swell of her derriere. Only the sensation of his whisper against the shell of her ear brought her attention back to his lips. Full lips. Lips that had a smudge of dark chocolate nestled in the corner.

"My sister did the debutante thing. She needed a partner and Dad had two left feet, so I was drafted."

He maneuvered her into a complicated twirl, which surprisingly, she followed with ease. For the briefest instant, she forgot about licking that chocolate away and enjoyed the heady feel of his strong arms and the soft summer breeze encircling her body.

Such a decadent, simple pleasure—dancing. On second thought, while waltzing with Noah was decadent to the nth degree, *simple* it wasn't.

Miranda tried desperately to deny how snugly her hand fit in his or how his shoulder sloped at just the right angle to pillow her cheek had she the nerve to lay it there. Luckily for both of them, Miranda's willpower, while weakened, remained intact. She wasn't about to embarrass him or herself by acting like a lovesick schoolgirl.

"You're teaching talents aren't limited to psychology," she told him. "I never thought I could dance like this. My parents used to dance the waltz every year on their anniversary. I always thought it was sweet."

"Don't credit the teacher. You have an innate sense of movement. You must have taken dance lessons as a child."

"Me? No, that was Teri's domain. Ballet. Tap. Jazz. Drama. Recitals. I was the queen of the science fair. A biology summer camp junkie. I remember the counselors trying to arrange a dance once, but we ended up spiking the punch with a harmless compound that would have made an angry skunk smell like Chanel Number Five."

"What about when you were older?"

Miranda smiled ruefully. "I was sixteen at the time."

Maybe she shouldn't be telling him all this. Hadn't Teri told her something about being coy? About not saying the first thing that occurred to her? Lord, she was torturing herself enough by allowing Noah to hold her so close. She was quite sure she couldn't manage to curb *all* her impulses in one shot.

The music stopped and the two other couples disappeared inside. The band abandoned their instruments and the lights in the main dining hall and library flickered, signaling the imminent serving of dinner.

"I guess we should go in," Miranda said.

"I don't know. Amelia did suggest we skip the first two courses."

"She just awarded you the grant you wanted. I don't think she meant for us to absent ourselves completely from the dinner table and miss the announcement. Besides, I don't want Katie getting the wrong idea."

"You worry a lot about what other people think about you."

"It's an arrogant fallacy to believe that what other people think doesn't matter. This world is made up of 'other people' and they daily make decisions, based on their judgments, that affect our lives."

Noah's face skewed in disbelief. "That sounded like a quote from one of your articles."

She hesitated, then answered quietly, "It was."

"Well, I'm a firm believer in not believing everything you read—or write."

The dining hall filled quickly. Katie somehow finagled a seat immediately to Amelia Henson's right and she waved her fingerless gloves at Miranda and Noah. When they arrived, they found place cards with their names. Miranda, to Katie's right; Noah, on the other side of Mrs. Henson.

"She's fascinating." Katie did her best imitation of a subtle whisper, but Mrs. Henson smiled and patted her on the hand.

"You're very interesting yourself, my dear. Did you enjoy the dancing, Dr. Carpenter?"

Miranda blushed. She couldn't help herself. The

innocent question reinvigorated the warm glow she'd felt while secure in Noah's arms, following his lead, not worrying about who was watching or what they thought. She tried to recover by taking a sip from her water glass, but Mrs. Henson smiled knowingly and turned to Noah.

"That answers my question. You're off to a good start, young man. Just remember, the object of this experiment is to celebrate virtue, not destroy it."

"I'm well aware of that, Mrs. Henson."

"Yes, well, I can see that."

After tapping her wineglass with a silver butter knife, Mrs. Henson altered her knowing smile into a friendly one and welcomed her guests to her home. She spoke briefly about the cause she was raising money for this evening, then announced Noah as the latest recipient of the Henson Grant. Without warning, she invited Noah to give a brief overview of his hypothesis and research goals, which he did with all the eloquence and casual style Miranda admired so much in him. If he wasn't so terribly wrong for her, she was certain they'd be perfect together.

As the first course arrived, Miranda wondered how a man from an admittedly happy family could avoid commitment so staunchly. Every once in a while, something happened to remind her of how little she knew about him. He was married once. He told her that a long time ago. He turned down a fast track to tenure, preferring to earn his kudos the long way. Nearly thirty-three, the man made a hefty salary, bolstered by textbook residuals and consulting fees, and yet he still rented a small apartment in a complex peopled with college juniors fresh from dorm life and on their own for the first time.

She wondered if that's where all the rumors had started about his love life. She wondered how many of the stories were true. She remembered all too well the images of college coeds sunning sans clothes at off-campus housing back when she was at the University of Miami. There was just so much a man could take by way of temptation before he gave in.

On the other hand, there was just so much a woman could take of the same. Glancing at her watch, she realized she had at least two hours left to grapple with her attraction to Noah. Luckily, if dinner progressed at the same leisurely pace these events tended to follow, they'd just be retiring to the salon for aperitifs when the clock would strike midnight and the limousine would return to carry them home.

Two more hours, most of it spent at a crowded dinner table.

She could handle that.

PURELY IN THE INTEREST of common sense, Noah instructed the chauffeur to drop Katie at her dorm first. While she'd quizzed them about their date for the initial ten minutes after pulling away from Amelia Henson's house, the rest of the trip she marveled and wondered aloud about their hostess. Noah watched, in complete amazement, as Miranda oh-so-subtly encouraged Katie's enthusiasm. Her ability to counsel young people defied his own experience as a psychologist. She gave advice in the guise of questions and normal conversation. By the time they pulled away from Alpha dorm, Katie was practically running up the stairs to start a story about how women of all ages can make a difference simply by caring.

"Do you think she remembers why she got this assignment in the first place?" Miranda asked immediately after Noah changed his seat from directly across from her to beside her.

"I wouldn't bet on it. We seem to be the least of her concerns. You work wonders for her, you know."

"Me? Thank Amelia Henson. Katie just needs a little direction. She's a smart young woman."

"You're a smart woman. And beautiful. And sexy."

Eyebrows lifted, Miranda swiveled in her seat. "You can turn off the charm now, Noah. Katie's not here. Though I have to admit, I think you did your own share of influencing her tonight. Her troubles with men run deep, but I'll bet between your attentiveness and Mrs. Henson's stories about her husband, Katie may change her opinion that all men are pond scum."

"Good for Katie. But I'm more interested in you, Miranda. Is that what keeps you out of the dating game? Some inherent distrust of men?"

Miranda glanced up from her lap, noting with relief that the privacy glass between the driver and the back seat was raised.

"I don't distrust men."

"That boy, the one Teri..."

"The one I slept with? His name was—"

Noah pressed his fingers to her lips. The sensation of his touch sapped her breath. Instantaneous sensory overload sent her sagging against the seat.

Noah didn't move, except to gently smooth the roughened pads of his fingers over her mouth, then up her cheek, finishing with the soft twirling of a loosened tendril of hair around her ear.

"I don't want to know his name."

Good. 'Cause right at this moment, she couldn't remember it.

His eyes caught the dim amber glow of the dome light. The barely visible flecks of blue slowly diminished as his pupils dilated. Miranda watched, motionless, as his mouth, just inches from hers, parted, and his tongue darted out to quickly moisten his lips. Was he going to kiss her? God, she hoped so. She closed her eyes and dug her fists into the leather upholstery of the seat.

"Look at me, Miranda."

His voice simmered like lava, stoking the hungry embers of need. Fever ignited from his touch. He trailed a single finger beneath her chin, lifting her face to his. The heat from his breath teased her. The scent of brandy intoxicated her.

Or was the sensation the effect of Noah alone?

She opened her eyes to find him only inches away. The minute their gazes locked, his eyes caught the spark of her secret desire.

"You're not as immune to me as I thought, are you?"

She tried to break the spell by laughing.

It didn't work.

"You're not a disease, Noah."

He cocked his head, as though considering the possibility.

She frowned. "Don't play the sympathy card, Noah. You seem to have a checkered past with women. I don't know much more than that, but I know you well enough to believe you didn't hurt anyone on purpose. Or by design."

"Faith in my good intentions can be dangerous. Intent isn't the only factor in determining culpability."

"You sound like a lawyer. And I don't like lawyers."

But, God help me, I like you.

He shrugged, but didn't release her. He remained still as stone, except for the continuous stroking of her cheek, first with his fingertips, then with his knuckles. Alternating his touch, the contrast of softness and hardness made her wonder about the rest of his body. Where was he soft? Where was he hard?

Did she really want to find out?

Noah slipped his hand around the back of her neck, twining his fingers into the wispy tendrils. "Your virtue is in serious jeopardy at the moment." He punctuated his warning by tilting her head so her lips were mere centimeters from his.

"Is that a fact?" Her words, nearly breathless, elicited a curving of his mouth that was probably a grin.

But she couldn't be sure. Just as briefly as the smile appeared, it was gone.

"Care to have me prove it?"

She swallowed to clear her throat of the muffled sound of untapped passion. *Don't do it, Miranda,* she pleaded. *For once in your life, back down from a challenge. Move away. You aren't Wonder Woman. You don't have a magic lasso to get you out of this one.* She knew with every ounce of logic she possessed that Noah Yeager wasn't a man to bet against. Or trifle with.

Or kiss.

Not even if a kiss was all she wanted—and it most definitely was not.

5

MIRANDA DIDN'T FEEL the car stop. The gentle thrumming of her blood raging through her veins mimicked the rumbling motion of the moving limousine. When the driver opened the back door, she jolted away from Noah. Startled. Relieved.

Disappointed.

"Thank you." She accepted the chauffeur's proffered hand, grabbed her purse and started for the front door as Noah stepped out behind her. She stopped midway acrosss her ornamental bridge. Just because she couldn't control her overactive hormones didn't mean she had a right to be rude. Noah had been a wonderful date—charming and attentive and incredibly enticing. She'd have plenty of sweet memories to draw on—if she made a quick getaway. Things would progress from sweet to downright steamy in a matter of seconds if she said the wrong thing—or worse, *did* the wrong thing.

"I had a great time, Noah." She raised her voice to be heard over the sound of the departing limousine. "Thanks."

"The evening isn't over."

He joined her on the footbridge, her wrap dangling from his fist. She fought the urge to grab it away. The filmy material looked much too provocative in his grasp, as if he could easily manipulate the lace into some sort of sensual tool.

Pushing the deliciously sinful thought from her mind, she turned on a confident smile and stood a little straighter. "It's late. I have things to do in the morning."

He took a step closer and with both hands, flipped the scarf around her shoulders. "What about the things you have to do tonight?"

"I'm going straight to bed."

One eyebrow lifted. He tugged her a step closer with the scarf. The lace chafed the back of her neck, reminding her of that moment in the limo when he'd pulled her closer and threatened her virtue.

"Don't you plan to unwind first?" he asked. "Have a drink? Undress?" His gaze took a leisurely scan over her body. "Get comfy?"

Lord, it was hot out! That's what she got for living in Florida, though she would have bet an entire month's salary the temperature had risen ten degrees just since he got out of the car.

That little delusion didn't last long. Her knowledge of sexual attraction and physical responses kicked in and she realized she'd never been so turned on in her life. By what? He'd barely touched her! Then he tugged on the lace again, drawing her in so close, the lapels of his tuxedo brushed against her breasts. Her nipples tightened. Heat suffused deep in her belly, then lower.

"I'm so tired, I might skip everything and sleep on the couch—in my clothes."

He didn't seem to hear a single word. His gaze, riveted to the bare swath of skin between her neck and shoulder, flickered with desire. Unconsciously, she twisted a fallen strand of hair behind her ear, then let her hand linger on the precise spot he eyed like a starved vampire.

"Oh! Congratulations on your grant. I bet you can't wait to get right to work. Mrs. Henson seemed really supportive. It'll be—"

"Don't change the topic, Miranda."

With nimble confidence, he brushed her hand away and slipped his there. He reconstructed the intimate position of his hand at the base of her neck, just like in the back seat of the limo. Except this time, no driver would come to her rescue.

"I don't think this is a good idea," she whispered.

"No good-night kiss?" His gaze locked with hers, caught the glare from the porch light then reflected a gleam of intense wanting that matched her own with vivid accuracy. She couldn't deny she wanted this kiss. She couldn't deny she wanted so much more.

But wanting and having were two different things.

"No. No good-night kiss." She tugged away the edges of the scarf, freeing herself from his hold. But she resisted stepping away. She wasn't afraid of him. She wasn't! "It won't stop there. You know that as well as I do."

His smile confirmed her suspicion. Noah'd had no intention of stopping at a kiss. In fact, she doubted the thought had even occurred to him. Men like Noah knew nothing of limitations or parameters. He wasn't reckless—that she knew—but once he decided to pursue a goal, he did so with no holds barred.

He took one step back. She was safe. For now. For tonight. Oddly, that realization brought her no comfort.

"At least give me something to cling to, Miranda." He ran his hand through his hair, mussing the soft strands to the wavy disorder that was his and his alone. "If not a kiss, then tell me—what is the last thing you do before you go to bed? Describe precisely how you climb beneath the covers."

"That's silly."

"Is it? Or is it just a little erotic? A bit taboo, perhaps? Come on, Miranda. Give me something to distract me during my long drive home. Something to haunt me as I drift off to sleep. Something to dream about."

Miranda couldn't believe he could be so bold. She couldn't believe *she* could even consider telling him how she turned off the bed-stand light only after she'd carefully arranged her five fluffy pillows. Two beneath her head. One at each arm. One between her thighs. He wanted her to paint him a picture—give him the beginnings of a fantasy—about her. Her!

"You're joking."

Noah frowned and dug his hands into his pockets. "Why do you find it so hard to believe that I'm attracted to you? Because you're not my type? What is my type, Miranda? Can you tell me that?"

She pulled her wrap tightly around her shoulders. "Not with any degree of accuracy. I have only rumor and supposition to form an opinion. That's not good enough."

"You bet it isn't. Let me tell you something about me, Miranda." He stepped back, completely off the bridge, and Miranda shivered from a chilled wave of cold withdrawal.

"Don't worry," he promised. "I won't give away too much. I wouldn't want to make you uncomfortable or bore you with tragic details, but I don't date my students. Never have. Never will. I want you to know that."

Date his students? Oh, she'd heard that rumor before, but she'd never believed it. Not for an instant. Some of the women he saw were young, but none depended on him for a grade. She knew which of her colleagues crossed that line, and without exception, those men, and women in some cases, thrived on the quest for power and control. Noah didn't need to seek out authority. He wielded it without a second thought.

"I didn't think you did. You have more ethics than that."

"You think?"

"Of course."

So far as she knew, Noah was reportedly very clear with the women he dated. No expectations. No relationships. And those limitations, while honest, went against everything she ever wanted for herself.

Miranda glanced over her shoulder at her front door, then to Noah's sporty blue car parked in the driveway. Inviting him in would be such a huge mistake. Yes, she wanted to talk this out. Explore this aspect of his psyche that fascinated her beyond words. Delve into the recesses of his heart to find the tragic circumstance that turned him away from love and romantic partnership.

But so much more about him fascinated her than the way his brain worked. Like the natural warmth in his touch. The spark of raw energy in his eyes. The perfect way his body molded into the slick lines of his tuxedo.

And tonight, in the sultry summer heat of a typical Florida night, under a blanket of twinkling stars reflecting like tiny fireflies in the waters of the pond beneath the bridge, she knew now wasn't the time for explorations—of any kind.

"Why don't you come over tomorrow?" she suggested. "I do yard work on Saturday and I could use the help. We could have lunch after."

Noah opened his mouth with protest written all over his expression, then stopped. "Yard work?"

"What did you think? This gorgeous lawn was the result of a service?"

He nodded admiringly. "Mmm. Miranda Carpenter in torn cutoffs and maybe a sweaty tank, her hands moist with dirt and skin sun-kissed. Quite a picture to send me home with."

Miranda couldn't argue with that. The man could turn even her mundane hobby into a potentially sensual encounter. Her invitation suddenly didn't seem like such a good idea, but she wasn't about to back down. He wanted her to "confront the conflict"? Fine. Then he'd have to do the same. On her turf, literally.

"Glad I could oblige."

"MIRANDA?"

Noah gave up ringing the doorbell and knocking after ten minutes. When he heard the whirring buzz of an electric trimmer, he figured she'd started without him. It was after eleven. He'd gone to bed with every intention of waking early and surprising Miranda with fresh bagels and coffee. He hadn't counted on such a restless night. When he finally heard his alarm clock, breakfast time had come and gone.

Settling on lunch, he'd stopped by his favorite deli on the way over. After stuffing his favorite sandwiches, salads and desserts—chocolate, of course—into a cooler, he'd headed to Miranda's on a thrill of anticipation he hadn't felt in years. For a minute, he'd almost forgotten his promise to stay away from women like Miranda. The kind who wanted happy endings. The kind who wouldn't settle for one night. Or even one afternoon.

But he hadn't forgotten. Not really. Taking her up on her invitation was risky business. She was already starting to get to him. He'd actually started to defend his life-style before she'd even accused him of anything. When she'd dismissed his reputation as hearsay and declared her faith in his good intentions, he'd experienced a subtle warmth that defied desire and ran counter to simple lust.

Risky business didn't begin to describe Miranda. The more he learned, the more he liked. And liking usually spelled disaster.

And yet, he couldn't resist. Last night's date, no matter how brief or crowded with other people, was the most fun he'd had in a long, long time. Surprised though he was to learn that Miranda was attracted to him, he felt relatively safe cultivating a deeper friendship with her. She wanted, but she refrained. She lusted, but she abstained. While hardly breaking a sweat.

Good girls. Gotta love 'em.

He followed a stone path around the corner of the house and nearly tripped over his own feet when he caught sight of Miranda at the farthest edge of the property.

Her cutoffs were much shorter than even he had imagined. The frayed denim edge skimmed just below her buttocks, revealing long, tanned legs. When she bent over to toss aside an errant branch, he witnessed a flash of lighter skin that made him instantly hard.

She wasn't wearing underwear. Unless it was a thong.

And from the cut of her tank top, there wasn't a bra under there either.

What was she trying to do? Kill him?

After trimming a perfect circle in the ground beneath a short, stubby palm, Miranda switched off the edging tool and coiled the cord around her forearm and thumb. She worked with confident precision—not an air of daintiness about her. Hadn't he called her "ethereal" once? What the hell had he been thinking?

Her skin shimmered with perspiration. Her hair, a tangle of twisted, dark blond strands and silver clips, was sprinkled with grass cuttings and bits of Spanish moss, as were her arms and legs. Her lips moved, as if she was singing quietly to herself. Noah grinned when he noticed the thin yellow cord connecting a palm-sized Walkman radio hooked at her waist to tiny earphones.

Just what kind of music did Miranda Carpenter listen to when she cut her yard? Mozart? Bach?

Ravel? He could hope.

He set the cooler under a tall shade oak and set about to find out.

She'd turned her back to him to pluck some weeds from the mulch around the palm. Unaware of his presence, she knelt down, bouncing almost imperceptibly to the allegro beat of the music, turned up loud enough so he could hear.

Disco music.

KC and the Sunshine Band?

"Shake your booty?"

Miranda spun around, lost her footing, and ended up, booty-down, in the dirt.

She yanked off the earphones.

"Noah! You scared me to death."

"Weren't you expecting me?"

She glanced at her watch, then turned her clipping-splattered face to him. "It's after eleven-thirty. I expected you this morning. I figured you decided doing yard work wasn't your ideal weekend activity."

He assessed her attire with lingering appreciation. The tank top, a jeweled shade of purple that did amazing things to her lavender eyes, molded to her breasts, accentuating a fuller and rounder shape than even her evening wear revealed. "This is about as close to ideal as I've come in a long, long time."

She scrambled to stand, begrudgingly accepting his hand. "Then you're late."

"Sorry. I had trouble sleeping. I brought lunch. I take it you finished all the hard work?"

Miranda stood and immediately backed away, giving him space to avert his attention from her tight, tiny, sweaty clothes long enough to notice the layout of the backyard. With an apparent conservation area behind her lot, the yard had no fence to separate the precisely trimmed and tamed green of Miranda's lawn with the wild growth of sea oats, palmetto, pine and scrub oak behind her. Using tall hedges on either side and canopies of weeping willow and camphor at strategic intervals, Miranda had created a private paradise in the middle of an ordinary suburb.

"Depends on how you define hard work. I still have the weeding to do."

"I had no idea you were so into plants."

"I wasn't before I bought the house. The previous

owner ran the botanical gardens at the university. He brought his work home with him, and I couldn't bear to let it go. He didn't move far from here, so for the first year he taught me everything I needed to know. I had no idea I'd enjoy it so much. It's very relaxing."

Miranda rolled her head to the side, then in a circular motion, stretching the muscles in her neck. Noah heard the gentle cracking and wondered how she'd react to a neck rub. He knew how he'd react—which is why he kept his hands to himself.

She looked past his shoulder at the cooler beneath the tree. "It's getting hot. I'll probably wait until tomorrow to finish. Did you say something about lunch? I skipped breakfast and I'm starved."

If there was one thing he admired in a woman, it was a hearty appetite.

"Roast beef or turkey?"

"Subs?" Her eyes lit like amethysts. "From Antronik's?"

He nodded. The Greek deli was a campus favorite.

"Roast beef, definitely." She stacked her weeding tools in a bucket. "And if you tell me you picked up baklava, I may kiss your feet."

Feet? A good place to start, he supposed.

"You'll just have to wait and see," he teased, confident that the carefully packaged squares of the Greek pastry—the chocolate variety—would buy him some serious points.

Her grin brimmed with curious delight. "Let me wash up. There's a picnic blanket in the laundry room, under the sink. Go through the sliding glass doors and turn left."

She started toward the far side of the house without a backward glance. Wash up? Outside? Flecks of cut grass blades, curls of gray moss and a coating of soil touched Miranda's skin from head to toe. This was something he wasn't going to miss.

He retrieved the blanket from the laundry room, as well as a fluffy but faded beach towel she kept beside it. Throwing the blanket on a lawn chair, he quietly followed the path she'd taken to the side of the house. He found her shoes, a beaten pair of Keds, tossed outside a seven-foot wall of thick hedge beside the house. The sound of water pouring on concrete lured him closer. Moving shapes and colors...denim blue, deep purple and tanned flesh stopped him dead in his tracks.

"Miranda?"

The name came out in a soft squawk. She didn't answer. He hooked the towel over his arm and walked around to the side opening.

The space was small. No more than a three-foot-by-three-foot square of concrete tiles beneath a spigot surrounded on three sides by the hedge. The fourth side, the wall of her house, boxed her in like a natural shower stall. Miranda had unwrapped a coil of garden hose and was washing off her hands and arms. Just a woman removing dirt from her skin, and yet Noah couldn't have been more aroused.

She looked up and saw him watching her. She

froze at first, looked away, then shook her head and directed the water flow against the top of her knees.

"I'll just be a minute."

Her voice was soft, barely audible. Swollen with discomfort and...need?

"I'll wait," he decided.

She looked up then. "Noah..."

I don't think this is a good idea. She wanted to say it, but the words sat on her tongue, refusing to budge. Hadn't she said something similar last night? Out on the front lawn when he'd tried to kiss her...when she'd wanted him to kiss her with every nerve ending, every fiber of herself that was female and yearning for the touch of a man like him? *I don't think this is a good idea. Think* was the key word. She was always thinking. She thought too damn much. If she gave herself the chance to *feel* every once in a while, she probably wouldn't be coiled up tighter than the hose right now.

"I won't move from this spot if you don't want me to," Noah insisted. "I'm just...watching."

Sweat beaded on his forehead. She would blame the sun, but the corner of the house was shaded. Private. No one could see them. No one *would* see them. If she let go. Dropped the pretense. Surrendered to the forbidden fantasies she'd denied for so, so long.

And for what? Some inflated line of morals even the purest of heart couldn't tow? Sometimes—just sometimes—she envied Teri's disastrous relationships and heartbreaking trysts. Even when helping her sister through the tragic breakups, Miranda longed to feel, even for an instant, a need so powerful that even her incredibly cogent common sense couldn't keep her from diving straight into disaster.

Like right now. Right here. With Noah.

His fists twisted in the towel he'd brought her. The muscles in his arms bunched and bulged, pouring potent fuel onto the passion already simmering inside her. What would it hurt to explore this attraction? Who would it hurt? Other than her, she couldn't think of anyone. And she could take care of herself.

The supervised date ended last night. She could honestly and forthrightly report that they had both conducted themselves with perfect propriety.

Noah glanced over his shoulder, apparently assuring himself of the privacy they shared. "Unless..."

He spoke syllables. One word fraught with endless possibilities. Possibilities that stole her breath. Turned her muscles into taut, electrified cords. Infused her veins with a thrumming beat that sounded like bass drums in her ears.

"Need a hand?" he offered.

She closed her eyes. Her heart hammered against her chest. Yes. That's exactly what she needed. A hand. Two hands. His. On her body. Smoothing away the grime and dirt. Washing away the loneliness.

"Yes," she answered.

"What?"

He dropped the towel. She couldn't contain a smile, especially when he nearly tripped picking up the striped terry cloth before it soaked up the water pooling on the tile. He didn't expect her to agree. She'd caught him completely off guard. She'd caught *herself* off guard! The thrill was delicious.

"Just hang it up. Here." She indicated a spot in the hedge that was thin. With the towel in place, even a neighbor stumbling by wouldn't see them. Not that her neighbors ever stumbled by. Hers was the only house on this side of the cul-de-sac.

The privacy of the property had lured her to spend more on a down payment than she'd originally planned. Now, that investment was worth every single sacrifice.

He hung the towel, then took the hose from her trembling hand. Water splashed down, tickling her ankles and calves with cool drops and splattering the front of his tan T-shirt.

"You're going to get wet," she warned him, watching with fascination as his shirt became saturated and nearly translucent, revealing the outline of taut muscle and sprinkles of dark hair.

"So are you," he predicted.

If he only knew. Moisture surrounded her, penetrated her. Between the perspiration from the heat, the water from the hose and her own intimate response to him standing so close, she was soaked through and through.

"That's the idea, isn't it?"

She started to turn around so he could begin with her back, but he grabbed her shoulder. "Wait."

He tossed the hose on the ground. "There's something I have to do before I touch you. And I'm going to touch you, Miranda, like you've never been touched before.''

She knew, physiologically, that it was impossible, but a sensation much like the ceasing of her heart-beat, made her dizzy. Light-headed. Luckily, Noah grabbed her cheeks, lightly, but with enough pressure to keep her standing.

His gaze focused on her lips, while hers watched his eyes. The blue in his irises darkened as his pupils enlarged. His lashes, thicker and fuller than she'd ever noticed before, fluttered in quick, successive blinks—as if he tried to wake himself from a dream. Slowly, he lowered his head, teasing her mouth with the briefest contact—the slightest caress—an intimate sample of what was yet to come.

He didn't waste another second. When he pressed his mouth to hers again, Miranda could hardly contain a sigh. Soft yet insistent, gentle but demanding, his lips coaxed hers to open with the most delicate of kisses. He tasted of sweet soda. He smelled of soap and sunlight. He felt like pure delight.

"I've been wanting to do that for a very long time." His confession broke the kiss, but not the hazy connection drawing them together. He massaged her cheeks with his thumbs, then plucked a dried leaf from a tendril of hair.

"I've been wanting you to do that—among other things."

The admission startled both of them, but Miranda couldn't turn back now. Kissing Noah had been a commitment in itself—the kind of commitment even he could live with. For today. For now, she wanted to know him. Really know him. Every inch of him.

And he would know her—in ways she barely comprehended.

Turning, she faced the wall and smoothed the loose strands of hair away from her neck. "Start here. I hate when I get dirt on my neck."

Neck? Why'd she have to start with the neck? Noah groaned. Yet when she glanced over her shoulder and met his frustrated gaze with soft, lavender promise, his muscles eased, then tightened with a different kind of tension. She wasn't torturing him. She was inviting him. To fulfill his promise. To help her wash.

To make her wet.

He kicked off his deck shoes and slid them out of the way. She turned her face toward the wall. He took a deep breath, then raised the hose until the water streamed down her neck and over her shoulders.

She squealed and jumped. "It's cold!"

A field of gooseflesh popped up on her skin.

"Then it should feel good. It's wicked hot today."

And it was about to get more wicked. And more hot.

A dark layer of dirt dripped away on the stream of water, but a few stubborn grass cuttings and grains of sand remained. He reached out the few inches that separated them and smoothed the trimmings away.

Her skin was hot to the touch, even beneath the

steady layer of water. She sighed when he made contact—and didn't retreat.

"You're right. This feels very good."

He directed the water stream across her shoulders, wiping her skin with his palm as he progressed, watching as the errant droplets fell over her shoulders and down her breasts.

"It could feel better."

She hesitated, but then glanced up and met his stare.

"Could it?"

He closed his eyes and willed all his self-control into action. She'd opened a door. Cracked a window. Provided a keyhole entrance into the private inner sanctum that was Miranda Carpenter. Not the professor. Not the dedicated scientist. The woman. The sexy, sensual being he knew she kept carefully and steadfastly locked away.

"This is just you and me. Alone. Two adults who've been denying an attraction for longer than either of us would care to admit. Am I right?"

Her hesitation lasted no more than three seconds, and yet Noah felt a lifetime pass.

"You know you are."

A single step and the gap between their bodies disappeared. His chest pressed to her back, the water from her clothes seeped into his. He couldn't hide his erection—and he didn't want to. She needed to know the breadth of her effect on him. She needed to know—before he crossed the line from friend to lover—just how much he wanted her.

"You can stop me whenever you want to."

He slid one strap of her tank top down her shoulder, then washed the length of her arm with the water and his hand.

"I know."

When the skin was clean, he placed a feathery kiss on the tip of her collarbone, then proceeded to bathe her other side. Strap down. Water cool. Hands smooth. Skin clean and kissed.

"Hold this."

He hooked the hose into her hand, noticing the gentle trembling that sent the water splashing against the wall. Glancing over her shoulder, he noticed her eyes were closed. He'd make her open them before he finished...before he brought her to the edge of climax then eased her over the brink. He yearned to see the wonder in her eyes. The newness. The freshness he hadn't seen in so long. Perhaps, not ever.

Suddenly, he felt very much like a student on the verge of discovery. Not the teacher. Yes, he had the knowledge to pleasure Miranda. And man-oh-man did he have the desire. But the confidence of experience dispersed at the sight of her sun-kissed skin, rounded shoulders and pouting lips.

He knew then that he was the one with the most to learn.

6

MIRANDA PRESSED the hose to her stomach as Noah unhooked her arms from the straps of her shirt, then eased the soaked cotton material down, leaving it wrapped around her waist like a belt. Her breasts, heavy with need and gritty with sand and sweat, swelled. Her nipples pouted, as if reaching for his touch.

When he stepped back to remove his own shirt, Miranda couldn't contain a groan of disappointment. His hardness pressed against the soft curve of her buttocks felt so right, so natural. Like a part of her that had been missing for a very long time.

Just as she started to chastise herself for silly, over-romanticized thoughts, she heard the sharp snap of his jeans, followed by the slide of denim on skin and then the rustle of leaves and branches as he tossed his clothes aside.

He was naked now. She knew it the very instant he stepped back against her. He was hot and hard, and yet cool and pliant. His body molded to hers, curve to curve, like the yin-yang in Chinese symbolism.

And she wanted to be naked too.

She nearly dropped the hose in her struggle to unbuckle her shorts, but Noah placed his palms against her belly.

"Let me."

He slipped the button from the hole and released the zipper with such leisure that Miranda thought she'd scream by the time he tugged her shorts down her thighs and over her knees. She didn't think she had the balance to step out of them, especially when he pulled her shirt down in the same direction. Wrapping his arm around her belly, he lifted her just enough to kick the clothes away, then retrieved the hose from her grasp before she dropped it.

Sunlight stole into the tiny opening between the eaves and the top of the hedge, heating the clips on her hair and the tips of her breasts like tiny flames of fire. She reached up and removed the bindings in her hair, then shook her head, gasping when Noah refocused the hose on her back.

"So soft," he murmured, following the stream of the water flow with his supple palm. He buried his nose in her hair and inhaled noisily—letting her know that her scent aroused him. He moved again, but this time Miranda didn't mind the absence of his body pressed to hers. Too many other sensations assailed her. He cleansed her with rapt attention to detail, introducing a new awareness to every inch of her body.

Down her spine. Across her hips. Over the curve of her buttocks. Cool water. Hot touch.

Miranda sighed.

With his thumb, he intensified the pressure of the

water. When the splashing stream met with the insides of her thighs, her knees weakened. He formed a brace with his arm across her midsection.

"Steady. I don't want to miss a spot."

She throbbed from head to toe, the sensation culminating at the apex of her thighs, a spot he avoided with both hand and water. "Don't miss."

"Don't plan to. Turn around."

She did so slowly, shyly. For a woman who was nude and sexually aroused, she didn't have much cause to be coy. But her emotions, a jumble of physical reactions and instinctual responses, beat her natural need for logic into submission. She didn't care what made sense and what did not. The only thing that mattered was trusting Noah. Learning Noah. Loving him—with her body, since her heart was still off limits.

When she faced him, he dropped one hand to his side, aiming the water at the ground so that tiny droplets tickled their toes. With his other hand, he lifted her chin so he could look deeply into her eyes.

"You are so amazing."

"No," she answered, shaking her head and sliding her hands up from her thighs to her stomach. A thin layer of damp sand came off on her palms. "I'm still dirty. And still aroused. You're not done, you know."

His irises grew dark as midnight. His pupils enlarged; his nostrils flared. Noah simmered with an inborn, feral hunger that beckoned to Miranda's simplest, most basic needs. She held her hands out. He washed them. One then the other, first splashing the water over them, then rubbing away the dirt.

Miranda smoothed her palm to her neck, closed her eyes and arched her back. He immediately aimed the hose at the base of her throat. As the water sluiced down, Miranda waited for him to touch her. When he did, she clenched every muscle in her body to keep from jumping out of her skin. His hands drew a path of wet fire across her shoulders, then between her breasts and across her belly, then back up.

He stepped close, his natural body heat competing with the warm sunshine showering them from above. The water bubbled between them. He cupped her breast so softly, she could hardly differentiate between the cool tickle of the water and the warm sensation of his fingers. Until he reached her nipple. There, he plucked her until she grew tight and hard—a pleasurable pinch unlike anything she'd ever experienced. She cried out and took a single step back so the wall of her house kept her from falling.

"Shh." He lifted the hose to her lips so the water burbled over her chin. "Thirsty?"

She lapped at the water with her tongue. "The water's sweet."

He bent down and lapped the water just as she did, their tongues flicking together. "You're sweet."

"How sweet?"

He drank the water that ran down her throat, slurping noisily as he sucked at her skin. When he lowered himself to one knee, Miranda slid her hands into his hair and guided him to her breast. Lapping the water over her taut nipple, he suckled and slurped and drank until Miranda cried out his name.

"Say it again, honey. Call me. Tell me what you want."

"Noah..."

He saturated her other breast with water, flicking the edge with his thumb so the stream of water hardened. He tweaked her first with the water, then with his teeth.

"Let me take you there, Miranda. Let me show you."

She couldn't think. Wouldn't think. Too many sensations assailed her. Delicious sensations sent quivers of need to the deepest part of her womb. Heavy and empty at the same time, the intimate space throbbed to feel him inside.

"Yes. Oh, please, yes."

She thought he'd stand and slip inside her, join with her in intimate bonding, but instead, he took her breast into his mouth and lowered the hose.

The minute the cold water met the swollen flesh between her legs, Miranda swallowed a cry. He meant to make her climax without him. She tried to protest, but he increased the water pressure and tightened his lips around her nipple, sapping her ability to speak, destroying her ability to think.

"Don't fight, Miranda. Feel it. All of it."

Tangible sensations of light filled her. She came with quick and furious tremors. Clutching the sides of his face, she tore his mouth away from her breast and pulled him up. He dropped the hose and smashed his mouth against hers—messy and awkward and raw. His tongue plunged into her mouth, renewing the swirl of desire he'd only just sated.

He breathed into her mouth, hot and hard. Which helped, since she was certain she wasn't breathing at all.

But she couldn't pull away. The unchained need—the coarse, immutable lust—grabbed her by the very essence of her womanhood. This man wanted her. This man wanted to pleasure her. And he had, in a way she'd never imagined. In a way that left him thick with unsatisfied need.

His erection strained against her belly. Pressing her hands to his chest, she felt his rapid heartbeat. The erratic pulse frightened her, but not enough to push him away—not enough to deny the sensations still running a mad course through her body.

Their tongues raged and fought. Miranda slid her hands up Noah's back, relishing the feel of taut sinew beneath slick skin.

A moment after she touched him, she sensed the slightest change in his kiss. His rhythm slowed. His breathing became choppy. He was pulling away. Far away.

If she let him.

Miranda knew she should let him retreat. She should insist he release her, get dressed and go home. They had no business seeing each other like this—touching each other like this—*knowing* each other like this.

And yet she couldn't deny the powerful, innately

seeded knowledge that loving Noah Yeager—outside, in the daylight, with only the sun and the leaves and the water as witness—was exactly what she wanted to do.

She slid her lips against his chin. "Don't stop, Noah."

"Miranda..." He spanned her buttocks with his hand, cupping one cheek, pressing her so close, she could count his heartbeats. "This isn't what you deserve."

"What? Do you think I need satin sheets? Soft lighting? Promises of love and commitment neither one of us can keep?"

Noah stopped his assault on her neck and slowly released her. She'd meant her claim as encouragement. She'd intended to assure him that she only wanted to make love. Nothing more. Such a declaration from her should have been music to his ears.

Instead, her words struck such a discordant screech, he reached behind him for the towel and wrapped the faded terry cloth around her.

"You want to go upstairs?" Her question brimmed with expectation.

"I think I should go."

He'd never seen Miranda look bewildered before.

"Excuse me?"

How could he explain this without sounding like an idiot or a cad? Reputation or not, Noah wasn't a man who rushed into relationships. Heck, he usually avoided them completely. But when he *had* taken the plunge—first into marriage and then into shacking up—he'd made sure to take his time. Go slow. Show some restraint with the women involved.

He couldn't treat Miranda with any less respect. "Please, Miranda. Seems I'm bound to spend the rest of my life apologizing to you. You deserve better."

He turned around, grabbed his shirt from the branch of the hedge and used the soft cotton to dry the water off his body.

"You're right. I do."

He fought the instinct to turn around. Her voice held no recrimination, no anger or regret as he expected. Instead, sultry tones turned her declaration into pure seduction.

Wet skin or not, he jumped into his jeans.

"This was...interesting," she continued. "Inventive, to say the least."

He wouldn't risk yanking up his zipper, so he pulled on his shirt and tugged down the hem instead. When he glanced over his shoulder, she was leaning against the wall, one hand clutching where she'd knotted the towel above her breasts.

"I want you to know..." His attempt at explanation came out in mangled phrases. "I didn't plan to...I didn't..."

"Have seduction on your mind when you came here? Don't lie, Noah—to me or to yourself. You may not have come here specifically to seduce me, but the thought hasn't been far from your mind for the past few days. I know, 'cause it hasn't been far from mine."

She kicked away from the wall and exited the private hideaway behind the hedge. He followed, watching with utter amazement as she walked away. With the easy moves of a woman completely confident with her body, nude except for the towel, she sashayed across the lawn, snatched the blanket from the lawn chair where he'd left it, then tossed the frayed quilt on the ground beneath the tree where he'd set the cooler.

Once she'd settled onto the ground and emptied the paper-wrapped sandwiches and side dishes from the cooler, she looked up. "I'm starved. Aren't you?"

He crossed the lawn, battling confusion with one-half of his brain, using the other to will his body to stand down. He'd never behaved so recklessly, so intuitively, with any other women. "Inventive" sex, as she'd termed it, was nothing new to his repertoire, but this time he'd acted on instinct, on pure, erotic intuition—as if he and Miranda were linked by something stronger than commitment and more permanent than marriage or vows of love.

But they weren't. Not now. Not ever. He'd be cruel to give her that impression.

"Miranda, I'm sorry."

"For what, Noah? For taking a risk with me? For pleasuring my body and then denying that same release to yourself? You're going to have to be more specific. But please, sit down and eat while you do it."

He couldn't restrain the smile that tugged at the corners of his mouth. She was Miranda, all right.

Back to business and straight to the point. Oh, and adeptly avoiding the most sensitive issue at hand.

"I know the contest means a lot to you," he said.

"The date was over last night." She unwrapped the roast beef sandwich on a buttery roll and took a huge bite. After chewing the mouthful into submission, she gestured with the sandwich. "You don't see any reporters running around today, do you?"

"Point taken. But I know your virtue means a lot to you. I have no right to attack your value system."

She swallowed her food, then reached back into the cooler for a caffeine-free soda. "Funny. I didn't feel attacked."

"You know what I mean."

She popped the can open and sated her thirst with a generous gulp that made him smile. He'd never pegged Miranda for the kind of woman who would relish the small pleasures life so often offered. Like good food. Dancing. Small talk. Heavy petting. He'd known her for three years, and yet, he now knew that he hadn't known her at all.

Her capacity to enjoy her body shocked him the most. He'd been telling himself for years that Miranda wasn't the ice princess others thought her to be, but only now did he realize the depth of his hypocrisy. Deep down, within the farthest reaches of his ego, he'd bought into the stereotype. She had to be frigid. Only that could explain the fact that she hadn't been attracted to him. Now he realized that Miranda was simply a master at tamping down her emotions—keeping her thoughts and feelings, even her most intense physical reactions, completely to herself.

"I did mean it when I said you're amazing," he said.

"Why? Because I'm not afraid of you?"

"You should be afraid." He grabbed the other sandwich and tore away the wrapping. He suddenly needed to do something with his hands.

"Tell me about her."

"About whom?"

"You pick. Your ex-wife might be a good place to start. Unless your mistakes from the past weren't responsible for you pulling away from me?"

No sense denying what was obvious. "Trish was a good woman—*is* a good woman. And a good wife. I was the one who screwed that up. She remarried a couple of years ago. Has a new baby, I hear."

"Is she the one who broke your heart?"

The question seemed absurd, but with Miranda watching him so closely, Noah didn't dare laugh. He bit into his sandwich with relish, trying to focus on the burst of fresh flavors rioting in his mouth rather than on telling Miranda how off base she was. His heart had never been broken, but he'd done horrific damage to the hearts of the woman he'd once hoped he could love.

She stared at him until he swallowed. She obviously wanted her answer.

"No one broke my heart. What are you really asking, Miranda?"

"You're the psychologist. You have a problem with

relationships. A serious enough problem that you stopped right in the middle of what probably would have been glorious, mind-shattering sex just to avoid starting one with me." She couldn't contain a chuckle as she popped open the plastic bowl of bow-tie pasta and feta-cheese salad. "The irony here is phenomenal. Here I'm supposed to be the good girl, and yet you're the one to put on the brakes."

Noah reached into the cooler to fish out the forks.

"You are good, Miranda. You're honest. You know what you want out of life." He tore open a second container of pasta and speared a mouthful with a vengeance. "Unfortunately, I'm not it."

"You're sure of that? 'Cause, hmm, don't know what changed my mind—" her sly grin was infectious "—but I'm not so sure anymore."

Noah stuffed the forkful into his mouth and chewed slowly. This was a topic he didn't want to discuss. Not here. Not today. Not when the scent of Miranda still surrounded him, when the texture of her skin remained more powerful than just a memory, when the sound of her climax echoed in his ears. For once, he was going to follow *her* preferred method of operation.

Retreat. And the sooner, the better.

MIRANDA LET THE SUBJECT drop. They finished lunch in a twilight-zone version of normalcy. He asked her about her lawn. She answered with more detail than he probably would have wanted on any other day. By the time the sandwiches, salad and chocolate-laced baklava had disappeared, they'd slipped back into that cordial rapport that Miranda was really starting to hate. When she'd gone upstairs to put on clean clothes, he'd left. She wasn't surprised. She wasn't even disappointed, which only added to the topsy-turvy logic that led her through the rest of the afternoon. She had a strange suspicion she might wake up soon and find the entire encounter had been the wackiest of erotic dreams. But that theory was shattered when Teri came knocking at her door shortly before five o'clock.

"I did miss all the Saturday cleaning and such, right? If not, I'll leave and come back later."

Miranda tossed a load of clothes into the wash, trying not to think about the Daisy Duke shorts and tight tank top she'd dared throw on that morning— ultrasexy wear that Teri had left in the spare bedroom during one of her many overnight stays. The image Noah had painted the night before had been too potent for her to ignore. When it looked as if he wasn't going to show up to help her, she'd donned the clothes just to see what it felt like. Out in the sun. Wearing next to nothing. She'd fantasized about Noah's reaction to her naughty outfit.

Only she didn't have to fantasize anymore.

Now, she knew.

"I'm done for the day. Wanna stay for dinner?" Suddenly, Miranda didn't like the idea of being alone for the rest of the evening. She'd much rather have something—or in this case, someone—to distract her from thinking about Noah.

Teri slipped into the kitchen and opened the refrigerator door. "What are you making?"

"Whatever Domino's can deliver."

"Pizza? Really?" She shot back to the threshold separating the kitchen from the living room, where Miranda flopped onto the couch and picked up the television guidebook. "Are you feeling okay? Did you start your period or something?"

"I'm feeling great, actually." And that was neither a lie nor an exaggeration. She flipped the pages to Saturday and scanned the science channel's listing. "I just don't want to cook or go out. You in?"

"Only if I don't have to watch a documentary on the mating rituals of sea slugs."

Miranda frowned and turned the page. "There's a musical on Bravo."

"Which one?"

"Hello, Dolly!"

"For Streisand, I'm in. Besides," Teri disappeared behind the refrigerator door again then reemerged with a jar of Calamata olives and a hunk of Gruyere cheese. "I didn't drive all the way over here to drop off this e-mail and leave."

"What e-mail?" Miranda grabbed the remote from beneath the newspaper.

"From my friend, Bernie, the one who works at WRMA in New Orleans." Miranda's blank stare encouraged further explanation. "I told you. She produces that radio health program that just sold to twelve new markets. I haven't seen her since we did

Equus together off Broadway, but she remembered me and said she'd be willing to help."

Miranda popped an olive in her mouth as soon as Teri twisted open the jar and held it toward her. "Help with what?"

"With your radio show."

"I don't have a radio show, Teri."

"No, but you should." Teri retrieved a chilled bottle of Chianti and two glasses. "You have a lot of good things to say to kids nowadays."

Almost choking on a hard olive pit, Miranda grabbed a paper napkin and spit. Oh, yeah, she had quite a bit to say to young people. But she didn't think, "Oh, yeah, now I know what I've been missing" was exactly the message she wanted to deliver to the public.

Miranda slid the Chianti to her side of the table and screwed off the twist top. "That radio show is just a pipe dream, Teri. Somebody came up with a goofy idea, pitched it and then I haven't heard another word."

Teri held out her glass. "That's 'cause you never call your agent."

"I have no reason to call LeAnn." Miranda filled Teri's glass halfway then did the same to her own. She had way too much on her mind tonight to risk alcohol-induced loose lips. "I'm not working on a book right now."

"No, but you should be working on your radio show. She followed up with the network yesterday.

Seems there's renewed interest. Speaking of which..."

Teri grabbed the remote, flipped on the television and punched in Channel 12. The local news was running a weather teaser, not Teri's usual viewing preference. Miranda didn't even know Teri knew when the news aired, much less that she watched it.

But her strange viewing habits were the least of her worries. Teri had that I-know-something-you-don't-know look on her face. The one that made Miranda nervous. Very, very nervous.

"When did you talk to LeAnn?"

"Yesterday. She said I could call her anytime and pitch an idea to her, so I did. Told her about that play I'm working on. Anyway, she asked me to give you the message."

"Why didn't she call me herself?"

"I sort of asked her not to." Teri handed Miranda the small cutting board with cheese and a knife, then at the last minute snatched the sharp implement away and cut several slices, checking her watch— *watch?*—twice. "I didn't want you distracted. Last night being your big date and all."

Whoa! There was a major subject Miranda didn't want to cover. She popped a slice into her mouth. "So how do you think this renewed interest came about?"

Teri sipped her wine and suddenly became fascinated with the detergent commercial playing on the television. "Seems one of the marketing execs at the network got ahold of the article on you in *The Bull Report*."

"You don't say?" As if Miranda didn't know who'd *sent* the article to said marketing exec. "I can't see how that would help. The article practically called me a fraud."

"Yes, but when you *win* the contest, you will be vindicated right back into role-model status. And as unusual as the contest is, the right moves on our part could ensure major media coverage. I mean, if there's not a war or a political scandal going on, the press loves this stuff."

Just as Miranda opened her mouth to respond, Teri started bouncing on the couch, scrambling to raise the volume as a local reporter known for her colorful pieces on wacky, homegrown news came on the screen.

"This is it!" Teri announced.

Miranda swiveled to watch, expecting Teri had roped the station into plugging her upcoming production of Williams's vignettes. When Miranda's photo—the same one that had appeared in *The Bull Report*—appeared in the square behind Yancy Graham's left shoulder, the words she recited, "professor of sex," "virtue," and "campus contest," all became a mass jumble.

Teri hadn't just called her friend in New Orleans and forwarded the article to the radio network. She'd unleashed the beast of the local media.

"Teri! What—"

"Shh!"

Miranda pressed her lips together and forced herself to listen while her mind registered and cataloged the bits and scraps of information she knew about producing a story for television. Her nomination wasn't breaking news. The report would have been prepared long before the evening broadcast. She was lucky the reporter hadn't shown up on her doorstep earlier today seeking an interview.

In a nauseating flash, Miranda imagined the reporter arriving around lunchtime, finding her reposing in a towel behind a tree, munching on subs with a gorgeous man in a sopping-wet shirt and an unbuttoned fly. Or perhaps, arriving a few moments before that and receiving no answer to her knock, the journalist's tenacity would have sent her exploring the property on the other side of the house, where she and Noah...

"It's a fascinating turn of events when a thoroughly modern woman takes a stand for virtue. More power to you, Dr. Carpenter. This is Yancy Graham, Channel 12 News."

Teri's squeal pierced the silence immediately after she punched off the power button on the remote. Miranda took a deep breath, slowly convincing herself that this could have been so much worse.

"Can you believe it?" Teri stretched her arms out, then plopped back into the cushions of the couch and folded them behind her head. "If I wasn't such a good performer, I really should have been a publicist. The network is bound to make an offer now."

As Miranda drained and refilled her wineglass, she

pushed the worst-case scenarios out of her mind. The reporter hadn't sought an interview—probably Teri's doing—and she hadn't discovered Miranda and Noah's tryst in the backyard and broadcast the lurid details. She'd had a two-minute mention in a local-interest report. Nothing to panic over. On a Saturday night, chances were that no one saw it, except for the radio network muckety-mucks that Teri had assuredly called.

No use in overreacting.

"You called the television station about me?" she asked simply.

"I directed Yancy in a dinner-theater production last summer," Teri explained.

With Teri's contacts, her potential as a publicist was impressive. But Miranda decided to limit her career advice to Katie.

"I suppose Yancy Graham is going to do a follow-up?"

Teri grabbed the wine bottle and topped off her glass. "She's going to bring a crew to the C.I.S.S. rally and report on the whole event. She's really psyched about the angle."

Miranda frowned. "Sex sells?"

"Does it ever. In this case, it's no sex that sells, but the outcome is the same. Of course, I'm assuming Dr. Noah Yeager didn't manage to lure you into his bed last night. That *could* change things."

Miranda popped a huge chunk of cheese into her mouth and shook her head. Nope. No siree. No bed. None at all. No Noah in a bed. Noah in her fantasies, yes. Noah in her backyard, doing wicked things with his mouth, hands and a garden hose. But nope. No Noah in bed.

Her virtue, depending entirely on the narrowest of definitions, was still painfully intact.

Teri remained silent. When Miranda finished chewing and swallowing, she had no choice but to elaborate. "Based on our behavior Friday night, I'm a shoo-in to win."

So long as no one found out about Saturday afternoon. And Miranda wasn't about to tell.

7

"NOT EVEN a good-night kiss?"

Katie Brown slapped her pen flat against her spiral notebook. "Man, either she *is* the most virtuous woman on campus or you are severely losing your touch."

Noah sat up straighter in his office chair. Katie might be new in the journalism game, but she obviously knew that a surefire way to the truth—at least with a man—was through his ego. She'd just questioned the potency of his prowess. Fortunately, Noah had spent the past thirteen years either studying or teaching about the nuances of the male psyche. He wouldn't be such easy prey.

With an even exhale, he eased back into the comfortable worn leather on his high-backed, swivel chair. "Dr. Carpenter is a true inspiration."

She jotted down his response, wrinkling her nose as she wrote. Katie wore her dissatisfaction, and just about all her other emotions, like a bright carnival mask. He wished reading Miranda was so easy. Since he left her house Saturday, he'd tried unsuccessfully to figure the woman out. She believed in commitment before sex, and yet she willingly participated in an erotic interlude that left Noah breathless even now. She claimed to be embarrassed to the point of utter humiliation after her sister revealed her private secrets to the world, yet she had lunch with him under a tree wearing nothing but a towel.

At least he'd learned one thing about Miranda this weekend, not counting the part about her being the most sensual creature he'd ever encountered. Miranda Carpenter wasn't as simple, straightforward or straitlaced as he'd once believed. Her behavior wasn't always based on black and whites. And if he once thought the gray areas would send her running for cover, he now knew that wasn't the truth at all.

She was a woman of myriad contradictions. And damn it if he wasn't hungry to unravel each and every one.

Katie tapped her pen point on her paper, reminding him she was still in the room. "I don't get it. What do you mean she's an inspiration? She inspired you *not* to make a move on her? I'm not sure that's a compliment."

"Trust me, it's a compliment." He swallowed the last of his coffee, wondering why he'd agreed to Katie's impromptu request for an interview. She planned to grill Miranda after class, but said she wanted *his* impression of the date first. The man's perspective. Truthfully, Noah could hardly remember what had occurred Friday night. His memories seemed stuck on Saturday afternoon.

"Katie, let me tell you something about men that you—and your readers—might not know. Most men really like women. We're fascinated by them. At a very early age, however, society demands a certain gender separation that breeds distrust of the opposite sex and heightens a masked curiosity often mistaken for disrespect."

She looked up from her notebook, her eyes, thinly lined by soft black, wide. "Huh?"

"Remember when you were little and the boys all played in one corner with their trucks and the girls in the other with the dolls?"

Katie shook her head. He shouldn't have expected her to have a traditional childhood experience.

"I played with the boys a lot."

"And how did the other little girls feel about that?"

She sat up straighter and ran her hand through her hair, which he suddenly noticed seemed a lighter shade of brunette than last Monday morning. And something else was different, though he couldn't quite figure out what.

With a hair-flip meant to show bravado, she answered, "They were jealous."

"Exactly."

She watched him for a moment. "I hate to ask you the same question twice, but—huh?"

Chuckling, he understood why Miranda took such a liking to Katie. She was starting to get under his skin, too. "When you were admitted into the 'enemy camp,' so to speak, your own gender turned on you. That's very typical behavior in children. I once did a study..."

Katie held up her hand. "You know what, let's try a different route. Could you forget, just for a millisecond, that you're a psychologist? Drop all the textbook babble and forget every study you've ever done and read about. All I want to know is *if* you wanted to kiss Dr. Carpenter. And if you did want to kiss her, why didn't you?"

He started to open his mouth, but Katie pointed the tip of her pen at him like a razor-sharp rapier. "Answer like a man, not a scientist. You use one word bigger than three syllables and I'm outta here."

Noah grinned and resumed thinking. He couldn't very well tell Katie, and thus the entire university community, that he hadn't kissed Miranda that night because he wouldn't have been able to stop there—a fact he proved to himself and Miranda the very next afternoon.

He shook his head. *Don't go there, Noah.* Not with Katie in the room. Not with anyone in the room. He'd made that mistake yesterday during the barbecue at his sister's house. As he'd stood over the grill, he'd allowed himself to remember, just for an instant, exactly what Miranda looked like wet and naked and enraptured. He'd relived the feel of her skin against his. The sound of her cooing as he laved her breasts. The pebbled hardness of her nipple between his teeth.

Not only had he burned the hamburgers, but his sister took away his spatula and interrogated him for the next two hours over the identity of the woman who'd distracted him so much that burnt meat and thick black smoke had hardly made him blink.

Only after pleading with his sister to give him

space, had she relented and let the subject drop. But not without one of her typical warnings. Something that amounted to, "This one must be special. Don't screw it up."

But Noah *always* screwed it up, starting with the high-school sweetheart he'd made his wife, only to make her his ex-wife just two years later. He'd thought he knew Trish as well as he knew himself. They'd been inseparable right up to the wedding day. But once they lived in the same house, shared the same bed, he found himself feeling more crowded than the candy bars he stuffed in his pockets.

He'd tried not to screw it up with Sarah either. After the disappointment of his divorce, he'd purposefully taken the relationship slowly. They'd been together for over six months before he finally gave in to Sarah's considerable sex appeal. He'd even held out for a few months more before moving into her apartment—which had been the beginning of the end—a long, drawn-out end that Sarah didn't quite accept until his lawyer advised him to take out the restraining order. When the job offer came from the University of Southern Florida, he'd jumped at the chance to start over. Be near his family. Forget all other personal relationships for a while.

He'd almost blown his vow when he'd first met Miranda, three years ago, but she hadn't seemed interested, and by taking up the practice he called random dating, he'd succeeded in keeping their interactions professional. But that wasn't the case anymore.

Not only was he now firmly ensconced in Miranda's private life—and she in his—he was talking about it to a nosy reporter.

Glancing at the partially closed door of his office, he looked for signs of his teaching assistant, maybe a student who needed to see him before class. Someone to conveniently cut this interview short.

The outer office was empty. In the background, he could hear the whir and sputter of the department copy machine where he'd just banished his grad student to make copies of his next exam. He'd find no reprieve.

He had to answer. *Did you want to kiss Dr. Carpenter? And if you did, why didn't you?*

"Those are tough questions," Noah said.

"Duh. Stop evading. Why didn't you kiss her?"

He wouldn't risk a lie. He felt certain he couldn't pull it off. He forced himself to focus on the night in question, ignoring the unhindered desire Miranda had revealed the very next day. "She didn't want me to."

"Did she tell you that?"

"Yes."

Katie sat up straighter. "That's ballsy."

"No, that's honest. Dr. Carpenter is a woman who says what she means."

"The old no-means-no thing?"

Noah squirmed. Not only did "no mean no," but "yes meant yes" in ways he'd never imagined.

"Dr. Carpenter made it very clear to me what her expectations for my behavior were. And she's the kind of woman whose expectations I want to live up to. Men like a challenge. Women like Dr. Carpenter up the ante."

Katie smiled in admiration of her role model. "So the playing hard-to-get thing really works?"

"Like a charm." Though Miranda had undoubtedly put a whole new spin on the age-old female ruse. Sometime last night during his restless battle with sleep, Noah realized that while Miranda had opened a gate to her body Saturday afternoon, the wall around her heart was still utterly formidable. She'd allowed him access only to the part of her she felt certain he wouldn't hurt.

But she'd made the mistake of whetting his appetite. Her body was a fine, cherished prize, but the contents of her heart, the depths and secrets of her soul, beckoned like the grail to pious knights of old. He just wanted a peek—a glimpse into what made Miranda *Miranda*. What fired her passions beyond the physical? What stirred her emotions to utter frenzy?

He probably had no business exploring that side of her. He'd put both of them at even greater risk if he didn't tread lightly. Yet he knew he'd never satisfy his yearning for her on the course he was now taking.

Time to shake things up.

Noah flipped his calendar to the end of the week, formulating a plan as Katie continued her questions.

"So, when do you lose your patience? Give up?"

He flipped open his phone book and jotted down a number. "When I win."

Katie's grin widened. "You sound awful confident. What if you don't win?"

Circling the upcoming weekend with a nearby highlighter marker, he wondered if he had lost his mind. He should stop this madness now, before he did something stupid—like believe he could become more than Miranda Carpenter's lover.

Yet, if he acted quickly, he might manage to snuff out this attraction before either of them got hurt. Not too quickly, of course. There was something to be said for fantastic foreplay.

"This is entirely off the record," he clarified to Katie. Time to end the interview and make some travel plans.

Katie clicked her pen and slipped it into the spiral coil on the side of her notebook. "Off the record."

He leaned forward. "I always win."

IF MIRANDA DIDN'T know better, she would have sworn she'd been set up. Here she was in the middle of her interview with Katie, and Noah miraculously appears in the doorway, his finger pressed over his lips, begging her to keep his presence secret. So, he wants to eavesdrop, does he? Not without paying a price.

"I'm sorry, Katie, what was your last question?"

Katie flipped back through her notes, completely engrossed in her work. With her back to the door, she'd spread her preprepared questions and tape recorder on the edge of Miranda's desk. They'd been talking for nearly twenty minutes already, but only now had gotten down to the real meat of the article.

"Dr. Yummy...I mean, Dr. Yeager said in class that he would provide the one thing your students face on every single date—temptation. Do you think he lived up to his promise?"

Miranda glanced over Katie's head and straight into Noah's intense gaze. Had Katie not been so engrossed with organizing her thoughts, she couldn't have missed the palpable tension.

"Depends on how you define *temptation.*"

That caught Katie's attention. When she looked up, Miranda broke her stare with Noah and met Katie's surprised gleam. The subject matter was obviously getting interesting.

"You define it." Katie laid her pen down, scooted the tape recorder closer to Miranda and leaned on her hand. "Now that you've been out with one of the sexiest men on campus, tell me what you think temptation *really* means."

Miranda eased her elbows onto the arms of her chair and steepled her fingers in front of her. With an imperceptible glance to ensure that Noah was still watching her, she brushed her index fingers against her lips. If he was going to play voyeur, she would make it worth his while.

"Temptation is finally knowing what you want...." She ran a hand through her hair, hooking the strands behind her ear, exposing her neck. Noah's gaze darkened. He loved her neck. He hadn't told her, but she knew nonetheless. "Yet, at the same time, temptation is knowing you can't have it. Not yet, anyway. Not until circumstances are just right."

"You and Dr. Yeager are adults," Katie pointed out. "Why can't you take what you want and say to hell with the circumstances?"

Miranda grinned. That was a damn good question. If not for Noah's wise choice to back away, the overpowering lure of lust had nearly led her to subscribe to that exact philosophy, despite that she'd railed against it for a substantial portion of her adult life.

Luckily, a good night's sleep and Sunday shopping with her sister—complete with the usual rundown of Teri's latest romantic disaster—reminded Miranda that she'd treaded dangerous waters Saturday afternoon—pun notwithstanding. She'd tempted all right...tempted fate.

Luckily, Noah had resisted. Why he'd resisted, she wasn't entirely sure, but thankfully, she wasn't insecure enough to blame any shortcoming on her part. Only a week ago, she thought he didn't find her attractive. She suspected he'd bought into the popular stereotype that intelligent, focused women—the so-called "good girls,"—eschewed sexual explorations because they weren't capable of enjoying themselves. Even she had feared that might be true. Now she knew without a doubt that wasn't the case.

And better still, so did he.

"Ramifications for your actions don't disappear once you turn twenty-one—or thirty, for that matter. In fact, the older you get, the more dire those ramifications can be."

"For example?" Katie probed.

"After a while, people become set in their ways. They become accustomed to the patterns in their lives. They get comfortable and...complacent."

"Young people are more daring and unpredictable?"

"It's more than that. You're more daring and unpredictable...and you expect your life and everyone in it to be much the same. When you're older, things like temptation have a tendency to throw you more for a loop."

"Did Dr. Yeager throw you for a loop?"

Loop? Miranda was still spinning like a runaway top.

"Why don't you just write that my date with Dr. Yeager was much more than I expected."

"Are you going to see him again?"

"I don't think so."

"Why not?"

"Yes, Dr. Carpenter, why not?" Noah stepped into the room, his hands shoved into his pockets casually, belying his steely stare.

"The contest required one date," Miranda explained. "You have your big research project to begin and, frankly, I was under the distinct impression that you weren't interested."

Katie nearly knocked her books to the floor. "Where'd you get that idea? I definitely missed something."

"You didn't miss anything, Katie," Noah assured her. "That assumption is completely out of the blue. I never said I didn't want to see you again. In fact, I came over here this morning to invite you out."

Miranda's eyebrows shot up. "Oh, really?"

He slid a sheet of fax paper onto her desk. She uncurled the message and read the text.

"This is a confirmation letter from the Don Faison Spa and Resort," she announced.

"Yes, it is. I booked us a suite for the weekend."

Miranda balled up the paper and threw it at him. "Well, unbook it."

"Why?" both Noah and Katie asked.

Miranda rolled her eyes. That was the second time these two had responded in unison and she wasn't amused.

"That's the most presumptuous, arrogant, egotistical invitation I've ever received! Don't you think progressing from one date at a crowded dinner party to a weekend away at a romantic resort—in the same suite, no less—is a big leap?"

"She's got you there, Dr. Y.," Katie concurred. "I think maybe dinner and a movie is more in line."

Noah removed his hands from his pockets and nodded. "Ordinarily, I'd agree with you. But as you two were just discussing, Dr. Carpenter and I aren't children. We're both very busy people. How many times do either of us have the luxury of going away for the weekend in the middle of a semester?"

"Busy schedules is no excuse," Miranda insisted. She resisted the urge to remove her jacket, despite her rising body temperature. A list of protests formed in her mouth, but each sounded hollow and hypocritical next to the fact that they'd practically made love in her backyard the day before yesterday.

She'd said no to his invitation. He'd go away now.

"I know you love the beach," he continued.

She should have known better.

"No, thank you."

"Why not? I told you, it's a suite. You'll have your own bedroom. Are you saying you won't be able to control yourself with me so close?"

He leaned over her desk, tempting her with his woodsy scent, challenging her with his insolent grin.

"One of the mistakes young people make is putting themselves into unwise situations."

"So you *are* afraid you won't be able to control yourself."

"I have complete command of my hormones, Dr. Yeager. That's not the point. Going away for the weekend with you is not the example I want to set for my students."

Katie had already started packing up her books.

"I think it's the perfect example," Katie mumbled.

"Excuse me?"

Katie clicked off the tape recorder and slipped it into the pocket of her loose-fitting jeans. "Under other circumstances, I'd say you were right. Going away for a weekend with someone is not a wise choice if you intend to stay...virtuous." She stuffed her notebook into her backpack. Obviously the conversation would now be off the record. "But the whole criticism of you in that first article is that you've kept yourself so completely out of the dating game that you don't really know how to play."

Slinging the nylon strap of her book bag over her shoulder, she eyed Noah from head to toe, then looked Miranda dead in the eye. "If you can keep your hands off Dr. Yeager after spending a weekend away with him at that ritzy resort, then you'll have proved yourself."

Traitor!

Miranda couldn't believe her ears. Katie was taking Noah's side? Encouraging this reckless, destined-for-disaster weekend at the bay area's most exclusive, most romantic beachside resort? Didn't Katie realize Miranda wouldn't be able to keep her hands off Dr. Yeager? Miranda knew that the same way she knew she had a class in an hour. The same way she knew that the sun would always rise. It was a fact. Pure and simple. Completely indisputable. Unavoidable.

"I don't think that's a good enough reason."

"Okay." Noah straightened the fax out on her desk. "Consider this. What if we were two colleagues going to a conference together?"

"They don't have conferences at the Don Faison," Miranda quickly argued.

"Yes, they do. You know they do." He smirked at her, daring her with gleaming turquoise eyes to listen to his argument. "Are you saying that two professional people can't go to a hotel together, enjoy the amenities and each other's company without ending up in bed?"

Yes, dammit. That's exactly what she was saying. When she was one of those professional people and he was the other!

"This isn't a professional conference," Miranda pointed out. She was avoiding the real issue and she knew it. "It's a weekend getaway."

Noah's grin practically oozed sly victory. "I thought you might say that. I spoke to the events co-ordinator for the resort. Seems this time of year, most of their clientele is over the age of sixty. I faxed her a copy of that article you wrote...the one Amelia Henson found so impressive. She was wondering if you might not agree to give a short talk. Oh, and she saw you on the news Saturday. Seems you're turning into quite the celebrity. She promised to invite that reporter, Yancy Graham, to the talk, as well."

He was clever. Very clever. Miranda loved the beach. She adored the Don Faison and she'd never turned down an opportunity for community service in her entire life.

And more and more, she'd been contemplating the real possibility of the radio show. While she'd never thought herself the publicity-seeking type, such a forum could allow her more access to the audience she wanted to reach. Most sex shows focused solely on feelings and emotions. And while she wouldn't ignore that area in the least, her unique perspectives on physiology might actually make a difference to people.

She sighed. His offer was remarkably enticing. And somehow, he even had Katie on his side.

She couldn't win. Unless...

"All right. I'd be delighted to be your guest, Dr. Yeager. But you'll arrange separate rooms, thank you. And Katie, since I've already fulfilled the contest requirements, I hope this...invitation will remain confidential?"

Katie smiled triumphantly and shrugged. "Do you see my notebook? The recorder is off, too, by the way. I do want a play-by-play when you get back—just between us girls." With a wink at her, and then, suspiciously, one at Noah, Katie disappeared out of the office.

"What did you do to her?" Miranda asked, incredulous.

Noah crossed his arms and leaned on Miranda's desk, watching Katie's retreat in stunned silence.

"She hated you a week ago," she said.

"Yes, she did."

"Now she's practically your partner in crime. Maybe I really am in over my head. Think you could give me a sample of that charm I could analyze? If I could bottle it, I could make a mint."

Noah's eyes drooped sleepily, as if he'd just woken up from a wild night of lovemaking. Or was just about to begin one.

"You'll get a healthy dose of me this weekend, that I can promise."

8

WHAT THE HELL am I doing here?

Miranda pushed away from the balcony railing, her movement jerky in contrast to the rhythm of the waves crashing on the shore below. Noah had walked her to her room nearly an hour ago, sweetly kissing her on the hand and disappearing down the hall without a backward glance.

She'd stood there for a full minute, hardly registering that he wasn't coming inside. He'd treated her to the most romantic of dinners in a private corner of the deserted hotel restaurant. He'd done all the ordering in advance, and the mix of textures he'd chosen—steamed oysters with sweet melted butter, chilled but spicy gazpacho, crisp duck à l'orange and creamy tiramisu—had whet her appetite for so much more. During the meal, he'd stroked her hand, fed her morsels from his plate, even insisting she close her eyes during that all-important first taste, then asking her to describe the flavors as they rolled over her tongue.

Miranda had never really been aroused by food before. Leave it to Noah.

He'd followed their sensuous meal with frozen brandy Alexanders at the quiet poolside. A few hotel patrons wandered in and around the area, but he'd again chosen a quiet corner where they could watch the stars with the pool lights behind them and the beach just beyond. The pulse of the gulf beating against the shore provided a rhythmic background for their quiet conversation about the constellations, mythology and the seductive qualities of the night sky.

And yet, except for holding her hand on their way back inside and then pressing his lips to her knuckles before he left, he'd done little but tease her with unspoken promises of what was yet to come.

And because of his behavior, Miranda was sure she wouldn't get a lick of sleep.

Slipping off her short satin robe and laying it over the balcony railing, she stretched, inviting the sultry gulf breeze to twirl around her body, fluttering the hem of her full-length nightgown. She'd thought for sure that Noah would be seeing her in that nightgown right about now. And it wasn't as if he wasn't interested. She had seen the dark shadow of desire in his eyes since the moment they'd met in the lobby. He was holding back. Keeping the lust in check. Making her wait. Probably waiting for her to beg him to touch her.

Well, she wasn't going to beg. He could get that idea out of his head.

But she was going to sleep with him before the weekend was over—that was a given.

The hour drive from North Tampa to St. Petersburg Beach had given her plenty of time to think.

During the week, she'd been able to hide from the topic by throwing herself into her work. She'd graded each and every one of her classes' exams the very day they were taken. She'd written an academic paper that wasn't due until next month and helped two graduate students with their theses, even though she wasn't their official adviser. She'd even drafted several topic sheets for her as-yet-unofficial radio program. But on the ride over, not even the CD she'd shoved into the stereo could distract her from coming to grips with the fact that Noah Yeager was so much more to her than a colleague. So much more than a friend.

And despite that they'd yet to sleep together, he was already becoming so much more than a lover.

She hadn't yet experienced the sensation of his body joined with hers, yet they were lovers all the same. Had been from that moment in her library when she'd fantasized about the nuances of his touch. Now that she'd experienced that touch, she couldn't turn back.

She was done with that. If she'd learned nothing else from the C.I.S.S. contest, it was that her days of hiding from life were over. She'd probably never admit it to Noah, but "confronting the conflict" was, without a doubt, much more satisfying than avoiding it altogether. She might be a damn sight more conflicted than she was a week ago, and a heck of a lot more confused, but somehow she knew that she wouldn't trade these experiences for all the misguided virtue in the world.

Though Miranda still believed in the strong moral code that helped her achieve her goals in life, she also realized that she'd used that code as a shield, protecting her from risking her heart. The time had come to make some revisions in her thinking, even if she ultimately lost Noah in the process.

Despite the cliché, she couldn't help remembering the sentiment her sister had once stitched—badly—into an overstuffed pillow. *It is better to have loved and lost than never to have loved at all.*

Miranda stirred the melted contents of her frozen brandy Alexander with her straw, then slid the cup back onto the small table on her balcony. She didn't need more to drink. She needed Noah, and not on just a physical level. She needed him because she was a woman—a full-blooded, warm-bodied female with needs and wants and desires. Yes, adults had a responsibility to be smart about relationships, but hiding from life was no life at all.

She knew that now. And by tomorrow afternoon, she intended for Noah to be in on her secret as well.

THE SPA ATTENDANT placed two fluffy towels, one for Noah and one for Miranda, over the carved bench. "Looks like you two lucked out," he said. "No one else is scheduled for the mud baths today. You have the whole place to yourself."

Miranda's head snapped up just in time to catch the twenty-something hotel employee winking at Noah. Leave it to another man to think he was behind their private interlude.

She'd called the concierge first thing this morning, asking about the amenities in the nationally known spa. After waking early with a renewed sense of purpose, Miranda decided that starting immediately after her scheduled talk and brief interview with Yancy Graham, the Channel 12 reporter, she was going to embark on a mission. Noah may have brought her to the resort this weekend to seduce her, but he was doing a damn poor job.

Time for her to take the reins.

She'd considered the hot tubs or massages, but they seemed...ordinary. She wanted a new experience to lead in to her new experience—the one she planned for this evening. The in-ground tub filled with a surprisingly sweet-smelling combination of clay, peat and hot mineral water, coupled with the intimate configuration of the room would provide the perfect prelude.

"Guests usually stay in the mud about thirty minutes." The attendant set a timer on the wall and then adjusted the stereo to pipe in soothing strains of jazz from the speakers mounted in the ceiling. "After that, you can shower here, and then through that door is a private mineral Jacuzzi bath. Another twenty to thirty minutes in there and then I'll be back to take you to the private blanket-wrap room where you can cool down. After that, you can do either a massage with one of our licensed therapists or take a refreshing dip in the pool."

The young man wiped his hands on his stark white resort pants, then gestured to a small refrigerator built into the wall. "Either of you like something to drink?"

When they both shook their heads, he wished them a relaxing experience and left, closing the door behind him.

"Well!" Noah's voice had escalated in volume just enough to indicate his nervousness. She couldn't help feeling a bit flattered. "This is cozy."

"Isn't it, though?" Miranda tossed her beach bag on a corner bench and slipped off her sandals. "In fact, an awful lot of this weekend getaway has been cozy, wouldn't you say?"

Except for the full house of thirty attendees and a camera crew at her talk this morning, Miranda had yet to see more than three or four non-hotel employees since their arrival. And now, in the warm, teak-paneled room, they were completely alone for the next hour at least. Miranda doubted they would once again get by with only small talk between them. Not when so much else begged to be said.

"I guess we picked the right weekend to come," Noah decided.

"How lucky of us."

Noah tossed his room key and wallet on the bench beside her bag. "Isn't it? This place is ending up to be worth the price I'm paying for two separate rooms— on different floors, no less."

Without the slightest hesitation, Noah shrugged out of his USF polo shirt and kicked off his flip-flops, leaving him in nothing but shorts. She'd seen his body before...just one week ago, to be exact. Still, the sleek, muscled planes of his chest, sprinkled with just enough auburn hair for a woman to slide her fingers through, stole her breath.

His hands slipped to his waistband, but he stopped when he caught her staring.

"See something you like?"

Miranda grinned. "Does that embarrass you?"

His eyes narrowed. He sensed she was up to something. Noah was many, many things, but stupid wasn't one of them.

"You know it doesn't."

She turned around and untied the sash on the robe she'd donned after changing into the spandex suit the spa provided for her to wear in the mud. "Good."

Miranda closed her eyes and held her breath, listening intently for the sound of a snap, then his zipper, followed by the gentle swish of cotton against flesh. She really didn't want to know what sort of wear the men were provided. Probably one of those tight little Speedos Olympic swimmers wore. She hated those.

She did. Really.

Except for possibly on Noah. She had a strong feeling she'd find him incredibly alluring in anything— including just a smile.

His decidedly male groan, only somewhat satisfied, caused her to turn. He lowered himself into the steaming pool of mud, his face a curious mix of enjoyment and perplexed disgust.

She couldn't help laughing. "How is it?"

He squirmed, settling into the curved bottom of the

shallow tub with his arms held high above his head. He stopped moving, but clearly wasn't quite sure of what to do with his arms. Finally he draped one, leisurely, along the side and folded the other behind his head.

"This is...interesting," he answered.

"Interesting how?"

Noah took a deep breath, scooting slightly lower in the goo with his exhale.

"Come in and find out. There are some things that defy verbal description."

Miranda had always heard about how relaxing and rejuvenating a mineral-enhanced mud bath could be. She'd only once allowed herself the luxury of a massage and a facial, and while the experience fully lived up to its decadent reputation, her life didn't exactly accommodate such frills. But up until last weekend, there were a lot of pleasurable experiences she'd denied herself. Now she was about to slip into a sensual pool of hot clay with nothing to look at but a view of the Gulf of Mexico and Noah.

She couldn't wait.

Situated on the fifth floor of the hotel, these private rooms were angled such that the tinted glass windows on the west wall gave bathers a clear, unobstructed view of the jewel-green gulf waters. Except for a few swimmers who'd ventured far into the surf and the occasional sailor of a sleek catamaran, no one could be seen from the windows. The sandy beach, close beneath them, was out of view. They were, effectively, alone.

Noah leaned back into the sloped edge of the mud pool and closed his eyes. Miranda quietly removed her robe and slid, literally, into the surprisingly warm combination of finely sifted clay and hot mineral water. As her bare skin slipped beneath the ooze, Miranda inhaled the heady scents of eucalyptus, camphor and several herbs whose mixture also proved heady, even if she couldn't identify them. The fragrance, earthy and warm, seemed to reach into her lungs. She couldn't help but relax, even when she caught Noah peeking at her slow descent into the mire.

"Comfortable?" he asked.

She was lying next to him in a tub of incredibly potent mud. How comfy could she be?

"I'm fine, thanks." Unlike Noah, she used her hands to guide her way in, ensuring that she didn't slip too close to him too soon. He lay just three inches away with only the mud between them. She submerged all the way to her chin.

"Looks like we're not going anywhere for a while," she said.

"Nope."

Miranda let the silence last just long enough to let Noah to consider that this wasn't such a bad idea after all. Her pores tingled. Her muscles eased. She could practically feel the rhythm of her heart slow to a lazy beat.

"This is a surprisingly sensuous experience," Noah commented.

"Mmm-hmm. The mud is so hot, and tingly—like a million little fingertips running all over your body."

He cleared his throat. "Do you mind? I'm not exactly in a position to make that particular fantasy come to life. Keep up the talk about fingertips and I might need years of therapy."

Miranda opened her eyes and turned carefully to the side. "Noah Yeager? In therapy? If you haven't done that by now, I doubt I'm the woman who's going to push you over the edge."

Noah laughed. "True. I've had my share of nutcases and you're not one of them."

"Neither was your wife?"

"Trish? No way. She was the reincarnation of Harriet Nelson, mixed in with a bit of Martha Stewart."

"Sounds like a perfect wife."

"She was."

If not for the fact that Miranda knew he'd initiated the divorce, she might have felt more jealous than she naturally already did. "Then why didn't it work?"

Noah stared at Miranda, unsure why she'd asked and equally uncertain he wanted to answer. They'd talked about his failed marriage before. Wasn't the topic closed yet?

From the intensity in her gaze, it clearly wasn't. Noah hated churning up his past this way. It accomplished little but reinvigorating his guilt over hurting Trish the way he did.

"The perfect husband I was not." He turned fully onto his back and stared up at the lacy blue patterns sponged onto the ceiling.

"Did you expect to be perfect?"

Noah adjusted his position. He was squirming and he knew it. "I wasn't even shooting for perfect. I would have been happy with mediocre, but I couldn't even pull that off. Do we have to talk about this?"

Miranda's smile was a distinct combination of self-satisfaction and sly design. "You aren't very good at confronting the conflict when it's your conflict that needs confronting."

"Conflict? I don't have a conflict. I don't have a care in the world."

"Oh, really?"

"Yes, really. Unless you want to share why you've kept yourself out of circulation on the personal relationship front?"

"I think I'm ready for that."

The admission made Noah forget to keep his arms out of the mud. He leaned to the side so he could see Miranda's face.

"Why now?"

"This seems like the perfect place for talking, for delving into the labyrinth of the human heart—even if you don't think so." With some effort, she lifted her hands to the surface. The milk chocolate–colored mud dripped from her bare arms. "Movement isn't exactly easy. Besides, it's private and we won't be interrupted."

He slid his hand toward her, not quite certain where the thick texture of the silky clay ended and her skin began. "Seems like the perfect place for other things."

"In the mud? Ew. I'd feel like a pig."

"I read a study once that said female pigs have thirty-minute orgasms."

Her eyebrows popped up, then narrowed over indignant eyes. "Forget it. I arranged this so we could relax."

"You didn't mind the dirt in your backyard."

She grinned and accepted his challenge. "What I didn't mind was the way you cleaned me. The water was so cool, your hands..."

"I remember, I remember." She was right. He wasn't about to attempt to come on to her in the mud. He had great faith in his abilities, but no man was a match for nature at its gooiest.

"Let's get back to you, then," he insisted. "You already know about my failed marriage, but you haven't mentioned any one horrible relationship that made you avoid the dating game."

She eased deeper into the mud. "Neither have you."

"I don't avoid dating."

"No, but you avoid commitment."

"That's because I have a long, ugly string of horrible relationships to convince me I'm not cut out for personal partnerships. Practicing psychology has taught me that some people simply aren't built for long-term promises."

She smirked, then forced the skeptical expression from her face. "Maybe I'm one of those people, too."

"You don't know. You haven't tried."

"You're right. But personally witnessing each and every one of Teri's disasters affected me in ways I don't think I even fully realized until recently. My sister is a beautiful, talented, amazing woman. Men adore her. Some of her boyfriends weren't even half-bad. And yet in every single case—even the ones where she broke off the relationship—she's walked away with a broken heart."

"Maybe your sister's too sensitive," he offered.

"Teri?" She started to object, but a single sidelong glance stopped her protest. "Okay. I'll concede that Teri is a rather emotional person. But that doesn't diminish the hurt she's felt. I've been there to pick up the pieces. I have been forever. And I guess after my one relatively rotten experience, I decided the whole process wasn't worth the trouble."

"See? There. We have something in common. Though, for the record, Miranda, you're not your sister. You'd make entirely different choices than she would."

"Would I?" Miranda looked at him pointedly. "She's been making goo-goo eyes at you since she met you."

"Her eyes don't excite me."

"But mine do?"

Since he had little to focus on at this particular moment, he could hardly blame anything else for the arousal he battled right now. Her eyes glittered like center-lit amethysts, but slightly bluer, as if they caught the reflection of the afternoon sky and held the azure hue just to drive him mad. The delicate fragrance of her shampoo broke through the strong herbed odor steaming from the mud; the sweet citrus scent teased him from the tangle she'd made of her hair atop her head with the same silver clips she'd worn last weekend. The image of releasing those clips and flinging them across the room, followed by a rather erotic picture of him brushing her hair, dried the moisture from his mouth.

"At this particular moment, it's your hair that has me hard."

She didn't even flinch. Darn her. For a self-avowed "good girl," not much shocked her.

"Do you always say exactly what's on your mind?" she asked.

"No, I don't." He turned back to staring at the ceiling before he did something really stupid. Like look a little too long at those curvy pink lips of hers. Or worse yet, lean over and kiss her—starting something he couldn't finish. At least, not here in the mud.

"Maybe you should."

"Be careful what you wish for, Professor."

Miranda remained silent for a moment, then replied in a voice so soft, so vulnerable, he wondered if someone else had come into the room.

"I'm wishing for you, Noah."

Her gaze glimmered with honesty—the kind that hurt, the kind that came with a price. Noah's heart clenched in his chest, then tried to hammer its way out. She wished for more than just another sexual encounter like their interlude in her backyard. She wished for something more intimate. More binding.

He nearly forgot to breathe.

"Miranda, I can't promise you I won't be any better than those guys who broke Teri's heart. My history speaks for itself."

"History is the past. This is here. Now."

"History repeats itself."

"When people aren't smart enough to see the patterns. Just admit you're scared, Noah. I will. You scare the hell out of me."

"Good. You should be afraid. Very afraid." Noah sat up, the rejuvenative powers of the mud effectively undone. He reached for the towel the attendant had laid along the rim and wiped off his hands.

"Then why did you bring me here this weekend? To a place you knew I'd love? A place brimming with romance and sensual experiences, if not to seduce me?"

"I did not plan to seduce you this weekend," he insisted, not needing her scoffing "ha!" to tell him the claim seemed ludicrous.

He had wanted to seduce her. He had wanted to ensconce her in an atmosphere so seductive, so arousing, she would remember their weekend fling forever. But that's all it would be—a weekend fling. A temporary liaison. No strings. He'd orchestrated last night to arouse her. Today—after they got out of the mud—he'd meant to follow through, but she'd beat him to the punch, and that alone threw him off kilter.

He'd considered, long and hard after his interview with Katie, how he could ensure that he didn't do to Miranda what he'd done to Trish and to Sarah. The answer came like lightning. He'd waited with them. Drawn things out. Acted as responsibly as he knew how—getting to know them before taking them to bed. In Trish's case, he'd even married her first. After all that time and emotional investment, the inevitable break-ups had done more damage than he ever intended.

So, with Miranda, he decided to start quick and end quick. Her responses to him in her backyard told him she was more than ready to become his lover. So he'd arranged the weekend at the beach, completely certain that they'd burn off the passion raging between them and then return to Tampa with wonderful memories of a liaison no one else would ever know about.

And while she seemed perfectly comfortable with that idea, he wasn't so sure himself anymore.

"I was wrong," he concluded. "You deserve better than a one-night stand."

"Well, we've actually been booked here for two nights."

"Miranda!"

"Noah!"

"This was a mistake." He scrambled out of the mud bath, flinging dollops of clay in her direction. He'd be damned if he'd admit it, but Noah cared about Miranda in a way he hadn't allowed himself to care about a woman in a long, long time. And that meant certain tragedy for her—the exact consequence she'd been trying to avoid for years.

He slid to the showers and turned on the water, wiping the layer of mud from his skin with long, hard swipes.

"Not so much fun when you do it by yourself, is it?"

Miranda reposed serenely in the mud, her eyes closed, her grin annoying.

He finished rinsing off before he answered, slipping out of his muddied swim trunks and wrapping himself in another clean towel. "I'm going to give you some privacy."

"Okay. But who was it that said, 'You can run, but you can't hide'?"

Noah didn't know the answer, and he didn't attempt to figure it out. Countless philosophers from Socrates to Bob Dylan could have penned that line. As he opened the door and left Miranda behind, he silently admitted only one thing—it was the truest sentiment ever written.

9

MIRANDA NEVER REALIZED how much hard work
went into an actual seduction. After she completed
the entire regimen of mud bath, mineral Jacuzzi and
massage, she ate a light lunch on the balcony of her
room then took a leisurely walk up the beach. Pam-
pered and primed from her time in the spa, she didn't
intend to waste all her newly buffed and exfoliated
skin. As she strolled past the small hotels and private
homes lining the waterfront, her plan formed. She
would make love with Noah, despite his ill-timed reluctance.

And though Miranda wasn't so sure about herself
anymore, she was certain one thing hadn't changed.
Once she made up her mind about something, there
was no turning back.

The journey to this decision began a week ago.
When she'd surrendered her body in the garden,
she'd honestly believed she could keep the confines
of her heart off limits no matter how far their lovemaking went. Actually, up until this morning, she'd
believed her powers of self-preservation were fully
charged. But listening to Noah admit, however
briefly and reluctantly, that he was to blame for the
failure of his marriage and that he still respected and

admired his ex-wife, opened her eyes. This was a man she couldn't help falling for, even if falling meant taking a risk. Like a skydiver jumping for the first time, she had to trust her 'chute—which, in this case, was woven with threads of insatiable desire and bundled by the regrets she'd feel if she let this opportunity slip away.

She wanted more than an orgasm, more than a roaring good time. She would connect with Noah tonight, truly connect, even if she had to pull out all the stops to do it.

When she returned to her room, she discovered a message from Noah on the hotel voice mail apologizing for his childish retreat. He asked her to go for a walk with him at sunset. They'd talk then, he promised. She'd left him a message agreeing to the walk, but left out the part about conversation. They'd done enough talking. It was time for action. Miranda made the arrangements with a girlish giddiness that belied her intent to be nothing but a full-blooded woman in just a few hours.

Luckily, Noah made himself scarce until a quarter before eight o'clock, the agreed-upon time for their rendezvous. Miranda found him at the edge of the pool deck, leaning against the gingerbread railing and staring at the gray clouds brewing a mile or so offshore. The threat of a full-fledged Florida thunderstorm sent most of the tourists inside, except for a few children shouting "Marco" and "Polo" in the pool while their exhausted mother begged them to get out of the water.

"Looks like rain," Miranda said, touching Noah's arm lightly to announce her arrival. Though painfully inane and cliché to start a conversation with an obvious observation about the weather, she didn't know how else to begin. *Hi, I'd like to go make love with you right now* seemed entirely too pushy, even for her.

"Want to cancel our walk?" he asked.

When he turned to face her, her ability to form even the simplest syllable fled. Her tongue grew thick and dry. Her jaw clamped shut. This wasn't the Noah Yeager she expected.

Something was different. His skin seemed darker, as if he'd spent the entire day in the sun. The ruddy tan contrasted against the whites of his eyes and intensified the blue of his irises so they shone with a lethal turquoise glimmer.

He wore his hair wet and slicked back, though it had dried just enough for a crown of waves to curl along the top of his forehead. Dressed in a light cotton shirt completely unbuttoned and his signature wrinkled khakis, he'd hooked his sandals in his fingers and wore a relaxed expression that contrasted sharply with the tension he'd exuded when he'd left her that afternoon.

Nothing in his physical appearance explained the subtle difference she sensed in him—a difference that made her heart clench in her chest so tight that her hands shook. But her attention returned to his eyes. Somewhere beyond all that blue was a man who'd made a decision. A decision about her.

She swallowed deeply and shook her head.

Good Girls Do!

"Let's go then," he said.

He slipped his hand into hers with a natural grace and innocent tug. And yet, not so innocent. The days of denying the attraction that haunted them were over. Miranda had decided last night that loving Noah would be worth whatever conclusion resulted. If she had her heart broken, so be it. Like Teri once said, heartbreak made her human. Heartbreak could yank Miranda from the ivory tower she'd hid in, behind her academic journals and impossible moral standards.

She'd needed today only to figure out the details.

Using his hand to keep her balance, Miranda leaned over and removed her strappy sandals. He took them from her, holding them with his as they stepped into the powdery white sand. He started to lead them north, but Miranda resisted. The only resisting she planned to do tonight.

"Let's go this way," she suggested, gently drawing him southward.

"There are mostly just houses that way. I thought we'd walk past that new hotel. Their margaritas are supposed to be outstanding."

She crinkled her nose. "I'm not a big fan of tequila. There's a beach house under renovation just a mile or so down. I want to look at it."

He raised an eyebrow. "Thinking of buying some gulf-front property?"

"I might—" she laughed, towing him quietly in the direction she intended them to go "—when the university triples my salary."

"Your house in the 'burbs isn't exactly a ram-shackle cabin."

When he followed her lead toward her destination, Miranda took a deep breath, releasing with it all her pent-up fears and expectations. She reminded herself that she could only plan so much. Most of what happened once they reached the beach house would be entirely up to him. Until then, she'd distract him with small talk.

"I indulge myself from time to time. I bought that house with the royalties from my textbook. I never expected so many universities would add it to their curriculum."

They talked about work a bit while they strolled, zigzagging closer to the water. The sand became wetter and flatter; ground seashells pinched the bottom of their feet until the rising tide splashed over their ankles then receded in foamy, rippling waves. The sun, effectively prevented by the clouds from setting with any degree of magnificence, instead gently faded, turning the sky from silver to gunmetal in fifteen minutes' time.

Not wanting to appear too anxious, Miranda stopped to pick up a large curled shell that had washed ashore. When the tide reached for her, she rinsed away the sand, then held her prize for Noah's admiration.

He turned the conch over, holding the shell close to examine it in the dim light. "I never knew you liked the beach so much until I read it in the newspaper," Noah admitted, handing the shell back to her.

"I bet there's a lot you didn't know about me until that article." Irony danced in her voice, surprising even Miranda. Her mind raced back to the afternoon in her garden. From the darkening of his irises, she knew he was remembering too.

"I've learned considerably more since then."

"Yeah? Besides the obvious—" she didn't even bother to avert a blush "—what have you learned that's changed the way you think about me?"

He reclaimed her hand before he answered. "In my professional opinion, I've decided you're crazy."

"Really?" She tried to match the forced seriousness with which he made his pronouncement. "Fully certifiable or just a little crackers?"

Noah held her hand tighter. "Fully certifiable, of course. This moment right here is a perfect example. You're taking a quiet, secluded walk—with me—toward a quiet, secluded house, wearing the sexiest sundress ever designed."

She glanced down at the gauzy peach wraparound she'd purchased at the spa. Nothing more than a long swath of cotton strategically twisted around her body and tied at the neck, she'd intended to use the loungewear at home where no one would see. But when she'd set her sights on an evening of seduction, she could think of nothing more appropriate—or inappropriate—to wear.

She flipped the short hem outward, revealing a generous sweep of bare thigh. "Too much temptation?"

"You've reinvented the word, Miranda."

They crossed in front of the house she'd been admiring—the one she'd called the listing real estate agent about this afternoon, the one that was still under construction and had no one looking after it.

A bit secluded, a bit public. They could be discovered at any moment. Miranda experienced that fantasy in action last weekend. Worked on her. Worked on Noah. She wasn't one to argue with a sure thing.

She tugged him toward the wood frame just as a crack of lightning flashed against the sky. "Interesting you should think that...but, trust me, I haven't even started reinventing that word."

Concrete-block steps led through a tangle of sea oats, weeds and brushy grass to the open doorway of the house. At least, she assumed it was the doorway. With the frame only partially enclosed, the layout was hard to visualize, even in the afternoon sunshine, when she'd first spied the perfect setting for their rendezvous.

"This is a renovation?" Noah eyed the empty frame curiously.

"Actually, the real estate agent said they tore down most of the original structure, except for a few interior rooms."

"You called about it?"

"Why not?" She stepped over a stack of two-by-fours. "I've made some good investments over the years. Maybe this is what I need for my retirement more than a fat IRA. Come on. I want to look around inside."

Lightning flashed once more against the sky, followed by a reverberating clap of thunder. The sound rolled over the open gulf waters, reaching a rumbling crescendo that made both of them flinch.

"This storm's a fast one," he said. "We should go back."

Miranda felt the first splashes of raindrops, blown in by the wind. *Mother Nature is definitely a woman*, she decided. She'd just been handed the perfect ruse to get Noah inside.

"Too late to go back. Come inside. The interior rooms are covered by the top floor."

She disappeared into the structure, traversing the lumber, drywall and blocks littering the floor.

"Watch out to the left. There's a stack of—"

"Ow! I see it. I felt it anyway," he muttered. "Miranda? Where are you?"

She had the decided advantage, having traversed the maze of construction supplies only an hour before. She'd set up her wares in the first solid interior room, which she assumed would be a kitchen judging by the configuration of pipes sticking up from the floor. She'd chosen a corner near the open doorway. After quietly fumbling inside the basket she'd brought over just before meeting Noah by the pool, she lit the quartet of ruby glass votives she'd picked up at the five-and-dime across the street from the hotel. The inexpensive quilts she'd bought warmed under the crimson glow.

She'd filled the basket with a bottle of Cabernet, an assortment of cheeses from the specialty shop beside the drugstore and two tins filled with a scrumptious meal, courtesy of the hotel's five-star chef.

Along with a supply of condoms and a special surprise for dessert, Miranda'd thought of everything.

"What's that glow?"

"Candlelight, can't you tell?"

"Where did you...?"

His question died as he crossed the framework that would someday be a doorjamb. He braced his arms on either side. He didn't move. The sky behind him had darkened from leaden gray to deepest charcoal. The wind kicked up, flickering the candle flames. His eyes, surely a shade darker than the storm, reflected the fiery gleam.

"Miranda?"

"So I planned this. Except for the storm. It's a nice touch, though, don't you think? Makes me believe in the power of Mother Nature."

To stop her nervous rambling, she popped the cork on the wine and poured. Her shaking hands sloshed drops of dark red fluid over on the crisp, new quilt. Noah knelt beside her and took the bottle from her grasp.

"You're shivering. Cold or scared?"

She closed her eyes as he laid his hand over hers. "Scared—to death. No, that's not true. Scared to life, if there's such an expression."

"You're right to be afraid, Miranda. I can't give you what you want."

She sat back onto the quilt and curled her legs beneath her. She spoke to her lap, not entirely sure she was prepared to confront those powerful blue eyes of his this close up. "All I want is one night to make love with you. Completely. No strings. No commitments. That's how you like things, so that's how it will be. Can you manage that?"

When he started to answer, Miranda realized she was using the wrong tactic. She and Noah didn't need to talk. She knew he believed he could never fully commit to a woman. She knew that for this one instance, his belief didn't matter. Yes, she wanted someone who would love her forever. Yes, she wanted to find one man who could fire her soul, her body and her mind with a single glance—a man who would be there for her for a lifetime.

But right now, she wanted Noah. Right now, he could be all that she needed, and more. And she could be exactly what he'd been searching for—a woman who shared his passions, but would walk away in the morning.

No matter how hard it was. She'd walk away. She'd made that promise to herself. And now, to him.

He meant that much to her.

"Miranda, you don't know what you're saying. You're not a love-'em-and-leave-'em kind of girl."

"No, I'm not. I'm not a *girl* at all—good or otherwise. I'm a woman, all grown up and, by now, pretty damn certain of what I want. Now, I went to a lot of trouble to execute this seduction." She lifted her arms beneath her hair, prepared to pull out every last stop if that's what it took to convince Noah that she could fend for herself. She didn't need his noble restraint. "You game, or what?"

ONCE AGAIN, he'd underestimated Dr. Miranda Carpenter. Grabbing her wrists with slightly more pressure than he intended, he kept her from lifting that glorious dark blond mane of hers. If she did, he'd feast on the sight of her lean, long neck in crimson candlelight. A man could only take so much.

"This isn't a game, Miranda," he warned.

"Can't it be? Not all games are trivial."

Her eyes gleamed like rare gems, a mix of amethyst color and opal fire. If he allowed himself the luxury, he could lose himself in those eyes. But he couldn't forget who he was or how he could never give Miranda the future she deserved.

"Every game I know of has both a winner and a loser. That's enough to keep me off the field."

She glanced at his hands, then dared him with those deep sparkling eyes to release her.

He didn't, which prompted her to gasp with frustration. "Noah, you don't have to be my white knight. Last time I checked, this damsel was not in any distress."

"You don't know—"

"Noah! Drop it. I know you hurt your wife when you couldn't make your marriage work. I know you hurt that girlfriend of yours when she wanted more than you could give. But as far as I see it, they have to take some responsibility for the failures. They obviously didn't know you as well as they thought they did. Maybe they asked too much. All I'm asking for is one night, maybe two. You, me." The sound of her voice, so throaty and deep and insistent, lured him to relax his grasp. She tugged free, releasing her hands and the top of her dress in one swift movement. "And the storm."

The gossamer fabric fell aside, peeling away from her body like a layer of translucent skin. Her nipples, dark and peaked, contrasted against the pale milkiness of her sweet, rounded breasts. His mouth watered in anticipation of tasting her again.

She reached out and cupped his chin, splaying her fingers along the entire side of his cheek, then combing her palm into his hair. "Sometimes, Noah, good girls do. And they 'do' very well. Let me show you what I mean."

Raising herself on her knees, she leaned forward and buried her lips in his neck. "Isn't this what you've wanted to do to me?" She murmured, nipping the sensitive skin along his throat, then soothing the line of nibbles with her tongue. "You have a thing about my neck. I catch you staring all the time."

"You have a beautiful neck."

"It's a fascinating fetish. Very Anne Rice."

Noah could hardly speak for the magic she wove just beneath his ear, but he didn't want her thinking he was some sort of sexual predator with a vampire fantasy.

"A fetish applies to someone whose sexual fantasies focus on that one area of the body alone."

She leaned back and bestowed him with a smile

that lit her entire face. "You're interested in other parts of me? Darn. Here I had this whole Antonio Banderas fantasy going."

"Antonio Banderas?"

"As Armand in *Interview with a Vampire?*"

"Didn't see it. Besides, I don't want you thinking about someone else when you're with me."

"Fantasies are healthy, you know that as well as I do," she teased, growing bolder the more he protested. She buried her face against his neck again, this time flicking the soft flesh of his earlobe with her tongue.

"Not when the real thing is better than the dream," he said.

She sat back and looked him square in the eye, her expression a mixture of seriousness and exasperation.

"Now, how the heck would I know that?"

"Have you forgotten last weekend?"

"Yes," she lied, her grin challenging him to remind her, bit by bit, in intimate detail.

He shook his head. "You're a regular pyromaniac," he said, knowing she'd understand his reference. She was toying with fire right now. The hottest fire of all.

"Better than a nymphomaniac," she quipped.

He laughed at her playful banter, hardly believing how her teasing was turning him on even more than her mouth against his skin. "How?"

"You know what?" She looked up, her eyes alight with amusement and flaming with desire.

"What?"

"You think too much like a psychologist. Anyone ever told you that?"

As a matter of fact, yes, he thought. But for the life of him, he couldn't remember who. Not with her tongue dipping into the shell of his ear, teasing him with a rhythmic caress so like making love.

He managed an "uh-huh," before she slipped her hands into his shirt and tore the material off his body, leaning him back into the layers of quilt she'd placed on the floor.

"One thing *I* remember from last weekend is that only one of us *really* had a good time." She leaned over him, her breasts heavy, her nipples erect and straining for his mouth.

"That must have been me," he answered.

Her eyebrows shot up. "You think that was a good time? You ain't seen nothin' yet."

10

NOAH GAVE UP the fight. Miranda was a grown woman with a will of her own. Needs of her own. He couldn't make her decisions for her and could only warn her so many times.

He'd allowed himself to believe that his experience with relationships made him some sort of expert. Time to turn the reins over to the novice. If she insisted on tangling with the likes of him, the least he could do was make it worth her while.

He'd suggested they take the walk to apologize for his behavior in the mud bath, to explain his reluctance for what it was—his desire to keep their friendship intact. But they'd already gone too far for that. They'd tasted each other. Felt each other. Experienced the exact kind of intimacy Noah tried so desperately to avoid—the kind Miranda was initiating now, leaning over him bare-breasted while making love to his ear with her tongue.

The storm outside intensified with the same rapid progress as the desire coursing through him. He'd never wanted a woman so much. Never. Not Trish, not Sarah, definitely not any of the forgotten many in between. Miranda was a class of woman all unto herself. Beyond beautiful. Beyond sensual.

He'd never resist her, so he stopped trying.

Grunting with a strange mix of resignation and exasperation, Noah splayed his hands on her cheeks and dragged her face to his. Blinded by heat, he kissed her, opening his mouth around her lips, swallowing her breath, savoring each and every taste, feeling each and every texture. The rain-tinged wind swept against them, bathing them in a natural moistness, cool and brief against the hot wetness bubbling from inside.

The candles flickered. A wineglass tipped, spilling crimson spirits over Noah's hand. Miranda laughed, straddled him, then pulled away from his kiss and drew his fingers to her mouth.

"Miranda..."

First, she licked his palm, lapping up the wine like a well-fed cat feasting on an extra helping of cream—slowly, savoring each taste. Then she suckled the curving valleys between each finger.

"Mmm." She saved his fingers for last, loving each and every one with her mouth while her eyes, dark plum in color and filled with desire, told him she intended to taste each and every inch of him in much the same way. He didn't know if he'd survive such blissful agony, but dammit, he was sure as hell going to try.

"I love your hands." She massaged his palm as she guided his hand toward the valley between her breasts. "So strong. So...skillful."

He reached to cup her, to pleasure her, to inspire that look of utter delight he craved on her features, but she stopped him. Her nipple was just a fraction of an inch from his touch and seemed to tighten with the heat of his hand, but still, she resisted.

"Do you know how much I want you to touch me?"

"I'm more than willing," he answered.

Her smile deepened. "I know. But not yet. I want to do for you what you did for me. Show you complete release. True pleasure."

She meant to punish him. Oh, she sounded all magnanimous and grateful, but this was about revenge—pure and simple. And if it wasn't, it should have been, because she'd devised a brand-new form of torture that was already driving him insane.

"I was wrong last time," he admitted. "I shouldn't have let you go alone."

She leaned forward, trapping his hands on either side of his head, brushing her nipples against his chest and smoothing her moist mouth against his. "No, maybe you shouldn't have."

Blazing a trail from chin to chest, she kissed and suckled and licked and learned every square inch of skin, every curve of muscle, every strand of tightened sinew. Every so often, she pressed her mons against his erection, reminding him of her final destination, of his final torment.

She plucked his nipples with her teeth before kissing away the sweet pain. She dragged her fingernails through his chest hair, straight down to the shadow that tapered beneath his waistband. While making love to his navel, she unbuttoned his pants.

Then she stopped. Leaning back on her knees, she tugged on his belt loops, waking him from the revelry of sensations of her mouth against his skin.

"Take these off."

Her demanding tone enticed him further. He stood directly in front of her and pulled down the zipper.

She sat back and watched. "Not so fast. We have all night, you know."

Noah took a deep breath and slipped his hands into his waistband. "Not if you keep staring at me that way."

She leaned forward on her hands, rocking on her knees like a tigress about to pounce. "What way?"

"That way. Like you've never seen a naked man before."

"Oh, but I have. He was a fine specimen, too. All lean and muscled and tan." She sat up and unraveled the rest of her wraparound dress. In seconds, she sat amidst a peachy puddle of soft cotton, like an angel on a cloud—a fallen angel, stripped of all things ethereal and untouchable and innocent. Noah nearly gasped, realizing that he now saw Miranda clearly—as a woman of great passion, a sexual being of incredible needs. He'd fulfilled that need before, but not to her satisfaction. Miranda didn't care only for her gratification, she wanted his pleasure too, as a part of hers.

She licked her lips. "He really had me hot and bothered."

Stepping out of his slacks and boxers, he knelt in front of her.

"Did he?"

"Mmm-hmm." She straightened so they were practically body to body, separated by nothing but the barest breath of a sodden summer breeze. Bracing her hands on her thighs as if to keep herself from touching him too soon, she raked her eyes over him with honest appreciation. "The thought of having him—of having you—inside me..." She met his gaze. "I can't imagine."

Noah took her fingers and lightly drew them to his mouth. Like that first night in front of her house—before he knew she wanted him with the same uncontrollable need with which he desired her—he brushed his lips over her knuckles. He loved the feel of her skin against his, inhaled her sweet ocean scent, so like the stormy smells swirling around them—and yet, entirely different.

"You don't have to imagine," he promised, "not after tonight."

Miranda smiled and diverted his kiss by dragging her hands down his chest, over his hips, then onto his erection.

"Neither do you."

With one hand, she cupped him, kneading so softly he wasn't fully aware of the building sensation until a groan escaped from the back of his throat. She encircled his shaft with her other hand, stroking him to a fuller length. Sensations at once new and yet as ancient as the wind, increased the pounding of his heart. He'd never felt so aroused, so intrigued.

So right.

If she hadn't eased him back onto the quilt, he might have pulled away. If she hadn't lowered her mouth to assist her hands, he might have torn off down the beach despite the raging storm outside. But she held him captive, enthralled, a slave to her intimate explorations. Noah couldn't run. He couldn't hide. Miranda offered her loving without him asking. Without asking for anything in return, except the intense pleasure of his touch. He could do nothing but take and hope, somewhere in the part of his mind that still subscribed to rational thought, that he could give as good as he was getting.

Miranda could hardly believe she could be so bold, but she trusted her instincts, acting on the innate pull of male to female to show her what to do. Hell, she knew what would please him. She'd read the books. She'd written a few. What she hadn't realized was how arousing *arousing him* would be.

Each of his guttural groans stroked her between the thighs as intimately as if it were his touch. Each breathless pant pricked her nipples to hard peaks. When he wound his hands into her hair, she loved him harder, deeper, wanting him to know the full breadth of her need. Somewhere outside the pounding in her ears, she heard him protest as she forced him closer and closer to the marvelous edge of climax.

Just as she tasted the first drops of his seed, he pulled her up against his chest and held her, viselike, for what seemed like a lifetime. His heartbeat raged in her ears as her hands slowly, lovingly finished what they'd started.

"I didn't want that to happen," he said, his voice ragged and resigned.

"Why not? It's exactly what I wanted."

"I wanted to be inside you."

"You will be." She rolled away from him, grabbed the soft cotton cloth she'd brought for their picnic, then walked to an open window and saturated the fabric with rainwater. She rang away the excess, then bathed them both clean.

He didn't speak as she washed him, and his gaze, so full of wonder and amazement, nearly squashed her confidence. She stopped once to fortify herself with a long draught of wine, sharing the contents with Noah when he sat up beside her.

"You've sabotaged me," he said, tilting the glass so she could take another sip. "I won't be ready again for at least ten more minutes."

She laughed, but didn't question his resilience. A man so full of passion, so completely sexed and sexy, wouldn't take long to replenish.

"I intended to buy myself some time," she said. "If tonight is all I get, I'm going to make it last."

Miranda didn't fool herself. She didn't have a Ph.D. and a membership in Mensa for nothing. Noah wasn't about to change his entire life-style just because of her. Any liaison after tonight would be like a promise he couldn't keep. Anything more than a one-night stand would spell commitment with a capital "C"—the same letter Noah would use to spell "choke-hold" and "chain." He hated that he'd hurt those other women. Too bad he couldn't yet admit how his own pain had him running scared. But at least she was beginning to understand his attitude. She couldn't expect him to change overnight.

She could only hope. Come Monday morning, they'd return to being friendly colleagues. But until the sun dawned, they'd be lovers without a care in the world.

Noah stood and pulled her up with him. "Then I'm going to make it worth the wait." He led her through the open doorway into the outer room, near the unfinished wall where the whipping rain pelted them from all sides. Hidden by the tall, swaying sea grass, a moving partition protecting them from prying eyes, he faced her toward the storm and stood behind her, his arms wrapped lovingly around her tummy and his strong thighs pressed against hers.

"Anyone could walk up and discover us," he whispered, dipping down and licking the rainwater from her shoulder.

"Only someone crazy enough to be out in this storm."

"Like us?"

She closed her eyes and leaned back into the rock-hard plane of his chest. His warmth surrounded her, battling with the chill of the falling rain. Her flesh prickled with gooseflesh and she knew he'd soon smooth it all away.

"Oh, yeah."

Lightning flashed, but Miranda only saw the glow

against the inside of her eyelids. The sensation of rain pelting her naked skin from the front and Noah nestling against her with his heat from behind was too delicious, too wonderful to stop. In moments, his hands wandered, one to her breasts, one between her legs. Soon she was gasping for breath in the same rhythm of the wild stormy wind.

"Oh, Noah, don't..."

"Don't make you come?" He twirled her around and pressed himself full and rigid against her. "I'm through letting you do that without me."

"Good." She leaned up and kissed him briefly, knowing she'd never break away, even to retrieve a condom from the picnic basket, if she allowed anything more than a fleeting touch of lips. "Wait here a second."

He tightened his wraparound hold. "Why? Need something?"

The sly angle of his grin told her he knew exactly where she was going.

"I need several somethings, if my instincts are correct."

"Hurry back. I want to make love to you right here, out in the open."

The thought thrilled her, putting a spring in her step that almost sent her tripping over a pile of PVC pipe. She grabbed a handful of condoms from the picnic basket and one of the lit votives for an extra bit of light.

She found him facing the beach, sitting on the edge of the unfinished porch, his back broad and rigid, his long, lean legs braced on the sandy ground. The rain poured with unrelenting fury. Lightning flashed only seconds before thunder followed. When he said they'd make love out in the open, he wasn't kidding. With only the tall, waving sea grass and the night's intermittent darkness to hide them, Miranda blew out the candle and ran out into the storm.

Without reservation, she swung herself onto his lap to straddle him, throwing her head back so the rain bathed her face and breasts with cold, sharp drops. Exhilaration poured through her in the same veins as her unadulterated desire for Noah. As if her skin could no longer contain her spirit, she felt as if she soared above the world with the rain clouds and lightning bolts.

But Noah immediately brought her back to earth. He combed her hair back then braced his hands on her shoulder blades, balancing her position so he could lap rivulets of water from her nipples and lave the curved underside of her swollen breasts.

Miranda didn't look down, didn't move, for what seemed like forever. She held herself still and enjoyed each and every sensation from his warm mouth alternating from breast to breast, to the icy rain, the swirling humid air, the strong brackets of his palms and the hot throb of his renewed erection nestled so close to her hungry center.

He nuzzled her neck, growling as his need matched the intensity of the storm. Shaking her head, she looked down through rain-splashed lashes to the gold squares of foil spilling from her hand.

He leaned back and waited, his eyes both dark with passion and alight with mischievous intent. He wanted her to put the condom on him. She gleamed at the unspoken challenge. Too bad he'd forgotten that she taught this particular subject in her advanced studies course. But this was nothing like rolling the prophylactic over the anatomically correct penis on her department-issue dummy. Noah was a living, breathing man. One with impatience in his eyes. One with desire written all over his body.

She ripped the foil with her teeth, then gently removed the transparent circle. The rain only partly hampered her progress, so she took her time on purpose, openly admiring him as she drew the tight material down.

"You do that very well," he commented, his voice as raspy and ragged as the thunder.

"I'm properly inspired." She drew herself up and ravaged his mouth while she slipped his erection between her legs, just at the juncture of her thighs. A riotous jolt of need brought a moan to her lips and set her body afire. She couldn't wait any longer. Her need to have him inside her, to share that ultimate intimacy, was more powerful than the waves battering the shoreline. "Be inside me, Noah. Please."

He agreed with a kiss. He didn't need to touch her to know she was slick and ready, and yet he slipped his hand between them to part her throbbing flesh.

She moaned again, this time with an air of surrender, and Noah felt certain he'd burst. He held his breath, focusing on her. He would feel the fiery release of his climax soon. But this time, he'd have the sensation of Miranda's pleasure to push him over the edge.

She was tight, but hot and fearless. Inch by slow inch, he joined with her, allowing her to set the pace with her hands braced on his shoulders.

"Take your time, honey. No rush," he urged, knowing if she went too quickly, he'd be the one that was lost.

She groaned and complied. He grasped her hips, noting with wonder how perfectly his hands fit on her body, how perfectly he fit inside her. He lifted her once, to increase the liquid friction drawing them together, then lowered her deeper.

She cried out his name.

"Let me see your eyes, Miranda."

Her lashes fluttered and her bottom lip was trapped with her teeth.

"I can't..."

With a grin, he dipped his head and took her nipple into his mouth, sucking hard until her eyes flew open.

"See? I knew you could look at me."

"If I look at you, I'll come."

"Honey, you're about to do that anyway. You might as well let me see it happen."

Noah wasn't one to back down on a promise, and Miranda shivered, knowing the ultimate payoff was just a few strokes away. He cupped her buttocks, kneading lovingly, then lifted her up and down, showing her the rhythm, teaching her the way.

She learned quickly. In moments, she locked her arms around his neck, drawing herself up so their noses touched. They didn't kiss. They hardly breathed. They just moved. Together. In sync. Eyes locked. The sensations building and building, reducing her breath to short pants, unleashing an aria of sounds from deep in her belly that urged Noah to lift her higher, to drop her lower, to touch her deeper than she'd ever been touched before.

"That's it, Miranda. Watch me."

He kept his eyes open, but the blue she'd once found flirtatious and sexy was all but gone, replaced by the dark navy hue of complete rapture.

"I'm just about there, honey."

She couldn't speak, certain she'd scream if she opened her mouth for anything but to breathe. Or to kiss him. So she did, hard and demanding, grasping his cheeks as if he were her lifeline. Her anchor in a surge of crashing pleasure. Her missing other half.

With one last upward thrust, Noah held her tight as their bodies quaked with ultimate release. Their kiss froze them in time, locking them together completely as sensations hot and intense poured from him to her and back again. Slowly, their mouths melted into a soothing play of tongues that brought them back to earth amid the dying storm.

THEY SAT THERE, entwined and enraptured, Miranda still joined with him, until the rain lightened to a shimmering sprinkle and the lightning was a silent strobe in the black night sky. The rustle of the sea grass, still swaying in the leftover gusts of wind, provided a soft music that helped calm their breathing and restarted Miranda's ability to speak.

"You're a man of your word, Noah Yeager."

He snuggled closer. Joking with her would be so easy now. So natural. But so ill-timed. After what they'd just shared, Noah knew he should be showering her with proclamations of love. Promises of many more nights even more glorious than this one. But he couldn't. Not when he knew quite well that his words would turn out to be nothing but lies. As much as he cared for her, as much as he adored her, respected her, admired her, he knew he couldn't love her for the long haul. He just didn't have the capacity.

Did he?

He shook his head, unable and unwilling to open that door tonight. If ever. He was a professional, for God's sake. He knew his own psyche. Too bad he wasn't so sure about his heart.

"I promised you a whole night of loving, sweetheart," he growled, nuzzling his nose into Miranda's hair until the sweet scent muzzled the sounds of his conscience. "Don't tell me you've had enough."

She lifted herself off him, then cuddled more comfortably into his lap, drawing her knees up and curling into his body. Her lashes fluttered, spilling leftover droplets of rain on her cheek. "Keep it up and I may never have enough of you."

For an instant, his heart halted. His emotions played on his face before he could stop them, but Miranda only smiled and kissed him—first his mouth, then each cheek, then his chin and neck.

"Don't worry, Noah. I'm not asking for more than we bargained. Take it as a compliment. When this weekend is over, I'll pine for you. Doesn't that inflate your male ego?"

Honesty came so easy with her, and yet he wasn't sure if she was joking or had somehow misunderstood. He grasped her chin and looked deep into her sleepy satiated eyes and begged her to understand. "No, Miranda, it doesn't. You know it doesn't. That's not what I'm about."

"I know, Noah. Believe me. I know."

As she kissed him, she slipped off the spent condom and set it aside, then laid her head on his shoulder. For a minute, he forgot all about making love with her again. He just wanted to hold her, caress her, brand her somehow in a way that was more than just sexual. Damn him for being so shallow. Damn him for being so self-centered and heartless. He wanted to love her. He could feel the swell of his heart as he held her, the possessiveness of his arms as they wrapped around her body. If he didn't know better, if he hadn't already been lured into blissful pseudo-love before, he would have believed Miranda had somehow broken through the last wall of resistance that stubbornly kept him from committing his soul.

But he did know better. Believing himself ready to risk more than tonight with Miranda wouldn't do either of them any favors.

He glanced over her shoulder, out into the churning gulf where white foam traveled over the tops of black waves and charcoal clouds glimmered on the edges from the hidden moon and stars.

"It'll clear up soon," he said, bringing her attention to the shoreline.

She moved to climb off his lap, but Noah allowed her only to turn so she faced the water too. He wrapped his arms around her middle and pulled her tight against him.

"Do you want to go back inside?" she asked.

The scent of her hair, rain-washed and drying into soft curls, lured him to bury his face into the downy blond mass. He grunted his disapproval at her suggestion, feeling the rumble of her chuckle with his arms around her belly.

"The rain's stopped. People will start walking the beach soon," she reminded him.

"No one can see us." The thrill of possible discovery sent his hands roaming. He spanned the length of her thighs from hips to knee, loving the feel of her weight on him. Drawing his hands back, he teased her intimate curls with his fingers.

When she sighed and reached behind her to grasp his waist, he continued his exploration upward to her breasts, skirting the sensitive undersides first, then cupping them full and greedily while plucking her nipples until she sighed again.

She leaned forward into his hands, lifting her bottom just enough so the growing moonlight caught the gentle slope of her lower back. She shook her head so her hair spilled forward over her shoulders and he kissed the sweet curve of her spine.

"You're driving me crazy, Miranda."

She scooted backward just a fraction, enough to make her desire clear. "That makes two of us."

11

THEY AWOKE CURLED together on the quilt and lay silently tangled as the sun broke in a cloudless sky. Miranda didn't say a word, not when she slipped away to use the construction site's Port-o-let, not when she splashed captured rainwater on her face and hands, not when she wrapped the peach-hued swath of material back into a dress.

Noah desperately wanted to talk to her, have a conversation, talk about the glorious night they'd shared, but he didn't know where to start. So he pulled on his pants, shrugged into his shirt and wordlessly started clearing the remnants of their trespassing.

"Ready to go?" she asked, hooking her hand into his as he leaned against the wooden frame.

He nodded, despite that he most certainly did not want to go anywhere. After a lazy walk up the beach under the first dawning rays of morning, they'd be back at the hotel. To pack. To check out. Out of the hotel and out of each other's private lives.

Noah knew it was wrong. He knew this parting would never last. Though they'd made love throughout the night, in the rain, on the porch, atop the quilt, they'd only scratched the surface of truly learning each other. He knew her erogenous zones. She definitely knew his. But more importantly, he now knew that Miranda read the works of D. H. Lawrence when she couldn't sleep, that her favorite color was any shade of orange, from apricot to tangerine, and she preferred her wines red and dry.

In between their lovemaking, they'd talked. Laughed. Gotten a little misty. About their childhoods, about their families, about the topics they'd never even touched on in three years of what Noah now knew were empty discussions. How much time they'd wasted!

And yet, as he led her down the steps and through the swaying sea grass to the beach, he realized they'd actually done themselves a favor. They'd truly created a night to remember. A night where every single second mattered, where every word and every touch and every look meshed into a picture neither of them would soon forget.

Miranda glanced at Noah through her peripheral vision, not daring to look him in the eye. She'd promised him. She'd promised herself. Desperately, she tried to pull together some anger at herself—even some at him—for making her break that vow by falling in love. But she couldn't manage so much as simple annoyance. Not when she felt—for the first time in her entire life—whole. Completed. Incredibly satisfied.

And yet, not whole, since she'd soon lose the one man she'd searched for all her life.

She watched the sand and shells beneath her feet, thankful that her hair fell loose about her face, hiding what she was sure was the bittersweet smile lingering on her slightly swollen, well-kissed mouth. He seemed content to scan the horizon and ignore her, except for the tentative hold he kept with her hand in his. She had no idea what she would do once they reached the hotel. Once he took one look at her, he would see that she loved him. She couldn't hide it. Not when the emotion made her heart brim to the point of bursting. She loved him—*him*—with all her soul.

And she couldn't tell him.

They strolled in silence. He swung the picnic basket wordlessly as they walked, watching the skyline as if he'd never seen the soft line of teal water blending into the pinkening sky. Miranda looked at the scene herself, one she'd seen so many times, and realized it did look different. Brighter, somehow. More glorious. Breathtaking.

And she knew why.

"I'm so sorry, Noah," she murmured, unsure why she felt so compelled to share her feelings when she knew they would destroy whatever friendship was left between them.

He looked down at her, perplexed. "Sorry? For what? For sharing the most amazing night with me?" He set the picnic basket down and wrapped her in a warm, yet somehow incomplete, embrace. "Miranda, what we shared..."

"Was incredible," she finished, burying her face

into his chest through the seam of his unbuttoned shirt. The breeze caught the sides and fluttered the white cotton behind him like a sail. If only they could harness that breeze and fly away. To another world—some distant deserted island where they could live alone and enjoy each other day and night forever.

But that wouldn't change a thing. Miranda would still love a man who didn't think himself capable of feeling the emotion in return—a man who vowed to stay out of a committed relationship for the rest of his life, and for the most valiant of reasons.

To keep from breaking her heart.

"Beyond incredible," he whispered. He slid a sweet kiss on her forehead, catching her breath. "So why are you apologizing?"

Miranda pressed her lips just below the curve of his throat, then inhaled, breathing in his scent, forcing it into her memory. Salty, like the waters of the gulf. And musky, like the essence of man. This man.

Exhaling, she resigned herself to the inevitable. Just as she'd told him the day before, she wasn't some innocent schoolgirl after her first sexual experience. She was a grown woman who may not have a plethora of liaisons to her credit, but she knew herself nonetheless. Miranda built her whole life on a foundation of honesty. She'd rarely lied to herself if she could help it, and she wasn't about to start lying to Noah.

She was about to come clean—and he was about to walk away.

Like a coward, she closed her eyes while she said the words. "I'm sorry, Noah, because I love you."

She forced herself to look up at him. As she suspected, his face was a mask of clay, not hard or stone cold, but unyielding all the same.

"I know I promised this would just be a fling. I didn't think..."

His eyes reflected nothing. His mouth opened slightly as if in shock.

She leaned down and picked up the basket herself, straightening to her complete height and retreating into the persona that had served her well over all these many lonely years. "But I'm thinking now, with my brain instead of my heart. You don't have to worry. I anticipate a little discomfort between us until we resume our usual routine, and that will require some time apart, but you have your grant and I have my classes. If we make a concerted effort, we should be able to adequately avoid each other until the feeling...passes."

He shook his head and glanced away, digging his hands into the pockets of his hopelessly wrinkled khakis. "Miranda, I—"

She held up her empty hand. "Don't say anything, Noah. I'm not asking you to. I'm not asking for anything. Life happens, as they say. Apparently, so does love. But it'll pass and I'll be fine." She emphasized those last three words, for his benefit as well as hers. She repeated them several times in her mind like a mantra before she spoke again. "It's not so bad, really. Kind of bittersweet." Nearly of its own volition, her hand gravitated to his. She touched his fingers lightly, relieved beyond measure that he didn't pull away.

"You're an amazing man, Noah. You've given me one glorious night...actually, two pretty terrific weeks. I won't forget that." She dropped his hand, knowing she had to say one last thing to smooth the way for when their friendship would rekindle. Someday. Later. Much later.

"But I will forget you."

She spun and walked away. Noah watched every step. He saw the tiny crescent her spin had left in the sand. Watched her footprints meld into the saturated white powder near the shoreline until she finally disappeared into the hotel.

She loved him. And damn his granite heart—he couldn't love her back.

Not forever, anyway. Right at this very instant, he loved her with every fiber of his being. He felt her absence like a hole in his chest, as if some unseen force had ripped out his lungs and left a huge emptiness all around his heart. He plopped down in the sand and dragged his hands through his hair, wishing he hadn't let her go, yet thankful she had the power and courage to walk away.

Miranda Carpenter loved him.

At least she said she did, and Miranda never said anything she didn't mean.

Noah buried his face in his hands, wondering what the hell was wrong with him. His mind slipped back, as if in a vortex of flashing time, to the day Sarah marched into his office with her therapist to tell him she was moving to Los Angeles and he could drop his restraining order. The triumph in her eyes had told Noah she'd finally exorcised the demon in her heart—him. Then he remembered the night he ended his marriage to Trish. He'd left, taking only his clothes and leaving divorce papers. She'd signed them promptly, attaching a handwritten message on a sticky note atop the legalese.

"If only you could have loved me back," it had read.

If only.

If only he'd loved her in the first place.

There he'd been, a noted psychotherapist—a man others looked to in their quest for secrets hidden deep in their souls—and he'd never looked deep enough into his own to discover that what he'd once assumed was love was really anything but. He and Trish had been children when they'd met, just starting high school. They'd discovered the wonders of hormones and sex together. They'd fought off the angst of adolescent loneliness by remaining true and committed and loyal. But after college, after they'd walked down the aisle and bought a home and even begun planning a family, the ugly truth came out.

Noah couldn't see a future with a woman he didn't truly know. The Trish he knew was fourteen and wide-eyed and uncertain of her place in the world. He'd grown and matured right along with her, but in his own self-centeredness he'd never truly recognized the woman she'd become. And when he did, she was no longer the woman for him. So he called it off. Just like that.

With Sarah, he'd never been so blinded as to believe he loved her in the first place. Theirs was a relationship brimming with sexual conquest and playful friendship, but lacking true substance. When the relationship ended, he'd been neither surprised nor disappointed. If she hadn't started stalking him, he probably would have put the affair behind him a long time ago.

Instead, he allowed his failures with Trish and Sarah to color his outlook on love and commitment in a particularly opaque shade of black. He decided he couldn't love anyone longer than a few months. He convinced himself that he couldn't envision his future beyond tomorrow.

He shut Miranda out of the place in his soul that seemed reserved for her from the beginning of time.

Noah was a coward. A fake. But admitting his faults in the privacy of his mind didn't change a damn thing.

Confront the conflict.

He'd written the catchy buzz phrase in his first published work. He'd preached the rewards of facing discord head-on for years. And yet, he'd never done it himself. Not really. He'd scratched the surface of his psyche just enough to dig himself into a neat, seemingly conflict-free life—when all he'd really done was bury his head in the sand.

And Miranda deserved a hell of a lot better.

"DID YOU SEE the article?"

Miranda looked up from the contract on her desk and smiled at Teri's sultry pose on the doorjamb. She wore a tight black leotard with long sleeves and a wraparound bodice, accentuating her lithe figure. Her skirt, a multicolored mosaic of see-through patches on a field of black crepe, swirled low to her ankles. She looked every bit the drama queen and Miranda couldn't resist smiling indulgently, despite that Teri was bringing up a topic Miranda didn't want to discuss.

"Yes, I saw it."

Teri seemed completely disinterested in Miranda's answer.

"Isn't this a great pose? Just once I'd like to be standing like this, buck naked, when some god of a man looks up and turns to ashes with hot lust for me. Some fantasy, huh?"

Miranda grinned and pretended to agree for the sake of expediency in changing the subject. The last thing she wanted to think about was hot lust and godlike men. It was hard enough to be back at work with Noah only two floors away, though they might as well have been separated by an entire continent.

After packing her small suitcase and calling the front desk to check out, Miranda had slipped onto her balcony for one last look at the gulf, one last memory of a night of loving he'd burned into her as if with a hot-iron brand. She had barely registered the midmorning humidity on her skin when she caught sight of Noah, still sitting on the shore, his gaze lost to some far-off point beyond the sailboats and Jet Skis skimming across the water.

She knew her confession would throw him, but she didn't think she'd leave him immobile. After feeling guilty for a split second, she slipped back into her room and grabbed her bag. Let him think about it. Let him stew. Maybe he'd finally realize that letting her go was the biggest mistake he'd ever, ever make.

If he didn't, then she'd be the one to admit the error of her ways. Never to him, of course, but to herself.

For falling in love with her eyes wide open and her logic slammed shut.

Teri abandoned her affectation and slid into Miranda's office with a swirl of her skirt. She closed the door behind her with a resounding thud.

"Speaking of godlike men..."

Miranda winced. She and Teri thought alike at the worst possible times.

"Sorry," Miranda said. "I don't know any such animal."

"Excuse me, but didn't you just return from your weekend getaway with Dr. Yummy? I only left twelve messages on your answering machine begging for the details."

She hadn't answered Teri's messages because she hadn't gotten home until late last night. Her agent had caught her on her cell phone just as she pulled out of the resort parking lot. The radio network had insisted LeAnn find her.

Teri's ploys had worked, though Miranda didn't plan to admit that until she'd delivered the signed contract. The show was a go, and she found a certain satisfaction knowing she could educate more people than just the ones who signed up for her class. After negotiating the entire afternoon, she'd spent the evening meeting with a producer, sketching out more topics and working on a schedule. Now, all she had to do was sign on the dotted line and she'd be on the airwaves from ten to midnight every evening.

Miranda fingered the top page of the legal agreement, drumming her nails on the network logo. It wasn't as if she had anything else to do with her evenings. Or *anyone* else to do it with. Miranda closed the contract, sighed, scribbled her name beside her lawyer's big red arrow, and jammed her pen in her university mug.

"As I said, I don't know any godlike men, Teri."

"Noah? Not godlike? Do you need new glasses?"

Miranda shook her head. "He may have Apollo's body and Zeus's charm, but I don't *know* him in the least."

Teri slid into the curvy chair opposite Miranda's desk and frowned. Her bright red lipstick against her pale foundation exaggerated the expression to exactly the point of heartbreak Miranda truly felt.

"Did he dump you?"

Miranda couldn't resist a self-deprecating laugh. "You can't dump someone you were never really involved with. We had a bargain. We'd have a good time, no strings attached."

Teri rolled her kohl-lined eyes. "No strings? God almighty, Miranda! Haven't you heard my sob stories enough to know that no such arrangement exists?"

"Sure it does. Adults have one-night stands all the time."

"Heartless adults, maybe. Shallow adults, definitely, judging by some of the losers I've caught sneaking out of my bed before the sun rises without so much as a 'thank you and what was your name again?'" Teri waved away the memory with a jangling flutter of hands, arms and bracelets. "You're not heartless or shallow. Neither is Noah."

Miranda scanned her desk, knowing nothing there—not the contract, essays, exams, books— would distract her or fill the growing emptiness inside. Even confiding in Teri would only ease the growing void for the moment. Only Noah could fill the widening vacuum—and that was about as likely as her sister letting this topic drop before Miranda spilled all the beans.

"Thanks for trying to help, Teri, but Noah and I have to work this out ourselves." She replayed that statement, then realized she was mistaken. She didn't have a damn thing to work out. She loved him. She'd told him. She'd definitely shown him. The ball was on his side of the net and he had to make the call on whether or not to return or take the fault.

"Maybe the article will help," Teri said. "Remind him of what a great time the two of you had together, of how 'perfectly balanced' the two of you are, according to your Katherine Brown."

Miranda smiled. She'd read the article more than

once since Katie sent her an advance copy by e-mail. Not only had her protégé skillfully described their date, but she'd captured the playful mood of the evening and done a bit of editorializing about Miranda and Noah's compatibility. Katie had somehow managed to tamp down her cynical side to create a wonderful piece on romance in the new millennium.

Too bad Noah didn't seem able to do the same. His cynicism kept him from seeing what Miranda knew to be true—they were destined to be together, if only they let destiny take its course.

She'd done her part. She *did* have her pride. Noah had to make the next move. "It doesn't matter who thinks we're perfect for each other, Teri, if Noah doesn't think so."

"Do *you* think so?"

A "yes" answer formed on her tongue, but then Miranda considered exactly what Teri was asking. Yes, she loved Noah. Yes, she knew they made very good friends and even better lovers, but did she think they were perfect? Completely compatible? Searching for the same thing from life and love?

Not by a long shot.

And still, she wanted him with every fiber of her being.

"Nobody's perfect. No relationship is perfect. Maybe searching for perfection is what's kept you from finding the right man." Miranda leaned back into her chair, resigned and spent. "Maybe it's kept me from even wanting to look."

Teri came around to behind Miranda's desk,

slipped her arms around her and leaned her head on her shoulder. Miranda clasped Teri's hands and tilted her temple to her sister's, wondering when the last time was that she and Teri had shared such a quiet, fortifying moment.

"See what you get for not looking?" Teri laughed and kissed Miranda on the head.

"Yeah." Miranda hugged her sister tighter, hoping the increased pressure would keep her tears inside. "I find a man who's so far from perfect, I can't resist him."

"DR. YEAGER, do you have a minute?"

Katie Brown knocked before entering. And if that didn't shock Noah enough to instantly wave her in, her new attire would have. He didn't disguise his careful inspection. She still favored the color black, but in a formfitting knit dress topped with a crisp denim shirt tied fashionably at the waist, she looked all college student—trendy, serious and confident.

"So, what do you think?" she asked, her eyes brimming with anxious anticipation for his opinion.

"The look suits you."

"Not the clothes!" She rolled her eyes. "Men can be so shallow."

She tossed her article on his desk. "Did you even read it?"

Noah scanned the folded newspaper, surprised he couldn't yet recite the words from memory. He'd gotten Katie's e-mail with an advance copy of her date review when he logged onto his computer after returning from the beach. He'd been surfing the Net for hours, aimlessly, until he realized he wouldn't be so easily waylaid from facing the demons he'd ignored for years. Katie's article sealed his decision.

In our generation, it's become commonplace to redefine words to suit our purposes and save our consciences from dealing with truth. But virtue has always meant conformity to a standard of right. *A truly virtuous person— woman or man—finds courage in holding themselves to that standard of right, however it's defined in their heart. A truly virtuous person doesn't settle for anything less but being true to their own soul. One brief night with Drs. Carpenter and Yeager convinced me that holding out for what's right can be nearly as thrilling as finally finding what you've waited for.*

Katie Brown had captured his conflict and held it up to him in stark black and white. Noah still didn't know exactly what his standard of right was—but when he finally found out, he was quite certain that Miranda Carpenter would fit the bill.

"You're a very talented writer. Dr. Carpenter definitely steered you in the right direction."

Katie swung her bag onto the chair and leaned on the backrest.

"Yeah, she did. I bet she could do the same for you if you gave her a chance."

Noah leaned back, certain he didn't want to discuss his private life with a woman barely out of her teens who'd only recently accepted the possibility that all men weren't liars, cheaters or thieves—no matter how insightful or inspiring her first shot at journalism was.

"Katie, I don't mean to be rude, but my relationship with Dr. Carpenter is no longer any of your concern."

She shrugged. "You're right, it's not. Neither is my childhood, but that didn't stop you from meddling."

He adjusted in his chair, certain his red hand was about to get caught in the proverbial cookie jar. "I don't know a thing about your childhood."

She dug her hands onto her hips and threw her head back for a hearty laugh. "Yeah, well, here I've been at college for two years and I didn't even know I *had* a counselor assigned to me. Then last week, she calls me out of the blue and, voilà, I'm her new project. She *says* one of my friends referred me."

"And you think it was me?"

"Her exact words were that I had 'conflicts I needed to confront.' Sound familiar?"

Noah smiled sheepishly. He should have just left an anonymous message for the campus counselor. But no, he had to go down and visit her personally, talk about Katie, tell her his theories.

"Okay, I meddled. Are you angry?"

Katie seemed to think his question over, but shook her head. "No. She's cool. She had a mom a lot like mine. Men in and out. Moved a lot. No 'strong male role model to give her a positive example of male and female interactions.'"

She gestured as she quoted, causing him to chuckle at the stuffy language his field often employed.

"I'm glad it's working out."

She nodded and rolled her lips inward while she looked him over with more wisdom than a girl her age should possess. He couldn't help but squirm a bit.

"I wish I could say the same for you, though. You look more rumpled than usual."

"Rumpled?"

"Yeah." Her laugh held a tinge of disbelief, as if she was shocked he didn't fully understand her description. "You've got that whole absentminded-professor thing going. It's very attractive to women who like that sort of thing...which isn't me, so don't get the wrong idea."

Noah chuckled again. Leave it to Katie to set that record straight. "Thanks for clearing that up."

"You're a good guy, Dr. Yeager. You deserve to be happy."

"I'm very happy, Katie. I have my grant, my work, good friends."

"Like who? Dr. Carpenter? Or is she more than a friend?"

He cleared his throat and restacked a pile of books he'd collected from his classroom. "Is this an interview? A follow-up article maybe? You knew about our weekend at the Don Faison. You wouldn't be here to dig for dirt, would you?"

Her eyes took on a tinge of sadness and Noah knew immediately he'd jumped to the wrong conclusion. Katie had never been a self-serving person. She spoke from her heart, acted on her emotions. She'd definitely come here to pump him about his time with Miranda, but not because of her job at the newspaper. Because she thought of them as friends.

"That was out of line," he said quickly. "I apologize."

"Good, 'cause I wouldn't use your relationship with Dr. Carpenter to further my own interests. I came here because I dropped by her office this morning. I didn't speak to her, though. I could see her working at her desk and the expression on her face just tore me up. Just call me a romantic at heart, but I thought you should know. You're all for confronting conflicts, and I thought maybe, just maybe, you didn't realize there was a conflict to confront."

"I realize it, Katie. The conflict is mine, not Dr. Carpenter's. And I'm working on it."

"Yeah, well, work faster." She picked up her bag and swung it over her shoulder. "I wasted a lot of time being miserable over things I couldn't control, over feelings I didn't want to deal with." Pivoting toward the door, she tossed her last piece of ironic wisdom from over her shoulder. "I'd hate to see you kids make the same mistakes."

12

MIRANDA APPROACHED the podium with a wry smile, a quick wave and a downright adorable blush. The audience at the kick-off rally increased the volume of their applause while she adjusted the height of the microphone with one hand and held tight to her plaque with the other. Noah tucked himself between two huge promotional banners—one for a campus ministry group and one for a popular brand of birth control pill—and watched the woman he loved accept her award as the Most Virtuous Woman on Campus.

He couldn't resist the swell of pride that surged through him—not because he had anything whatsoever to do with her win. If not for him and his "temptation," the award would probably hold a simpler meaning for her, though he willingly admitted that their lovemaking the weekend before hadn't lessened his respect for her one bit. In fact, his estimation of her virtue had increased considerably. She deserved more than a cheap wooden plaque for holding to her standards, especially around the likes of him.

Miranda believed in honesty. No games. No surprises except those most sensual. She told him she could have a brief affair and walk away. She promised that any heartbreak she experienced would only make her stronger. And it had—as well as more beautiful and infinitely more desirable, if that was possible. He'd watched her from a distance all week long, counseling her students, teaching her classes, even joking with her colleagues more readily than he'd ever seen before.

Every so often, he'd caught a glimpse of the sadness Katie'd oh-so-gently brought to his attention. From his office window, he'd watched her dash off to her car without an umbrella during an afternoon rainstorm, pausing next to his car just an instant before finding refuge in hers. But after the briefest flash of regret on her face, a sweet reminiscent smile had curved her incredibly kissable lips.

She was amazing.

"Thank you, thank you." Her voice boomed from the row of boxy black speakers in front of the stage. "I most humbly accept this award from the Campus Institute for Safe Sex, not because I think I necessarily deserve it, but because I truly believe in this cause."

The crowd quieted. While Miranda spoke, about half of the four hundred or so audience members continued to mill about, accepting literature and samples of everything from breath mints to music-store coupons, while the rest listened with rapt attention to Miranda's mellifluous yet forthright voice.

"The most important thing I learned from this contest—and yes, even people with Ph.D.'s often have a lot to learn—is that virtue is a misunderstood term. As Katie Brown so skillfully pointed out in her article, as we grow and experience life in ways that are sometimes sweet and sometimes painful, we can't help but define and redefine its meaning. But *virtue* is a word that can't stray too far from being part of our personal moral code—and I should mention here that if you don't have a personal code, you should. Decisions become infinitely simpler—though no less heartbreaking—when you set high standards for your heart."

Her words were crisp and businesslike, and yet Noah couldn't help but believe she spoke just to him. She scanned the crowd casually, comfortably, like the seasoned speaker she was, and yet, he recognized a slant to her smile that seemed private. Intimate.

He took a few steps forward.

"I'm a scientist, not a philosopher," she continued, obviously not seeing him, "so please don't expect me to wax too poetic, but I do have a few words to say about what I've learned about myself over the past two weeks since my nomination. I'll keep it short. I don't intend to bore you with the details—"

The crowd voiced their disappointment with a collective "aww," followed by a string of boos and hisses that made Miranda laugh.

"—but there are a few important discoveries I think are worth sharing. First, I learned virtue is best found in someone who has a clear picture of what they want out of life, though the picture will change, trust me. Second, when we get right down to the most basic definition of virtue, the archaic meaning is actually gender-specific. Big shocker."

Another laugh from the crowd. Noah couldn't manage even half a smile.

"For women, virtue meant purity. I'm not knocking that one, but in the spirit of honesty and reality and the sexual revolution, let me say that a woman is purest when she's deeply in love and loved in return by a man unafraid to show her the depths of his soul."

Noah stopped dead center in the crowd when Miranda finally found him. Her breath caught. Her eyes widened. Her mouth curved into that familiar bittersweet smile she wore whenever she looked at him.

The pause was personal, focused. The students immediately around him knew to turn in his direction, giving him the opportunity he'd sought all night— perhaps, all his life.

"What about men?" he shouted. "I don't think I'm quite clear on the meaning of virtue for my sex."

"Interrupting again, Dr. Yeager?" Miranda asked, her grin tentative but genuine.

"It works for me."

It works for us.

"Well, in men, virtue means courage."

He shouldered through the crowd as she spoke, never once letting his gaze stray from the direct line he had to her as he neared the stage. She hesitated briefly, then glanced at her notes once before folding them over on the podium.

"Courage to be honest. Courage to be discreet. Courage to be loyal and willing to risk heartbreak and disappointment and even humility to maybe, just maybe, find someone to share his life with."

He took the steps two at a time, shaking the temporary stage with his weight. He stopped nearly a foot away from her, afraid to get too close. He had the strong compulsion to wrap her in his arms and kiss her long and hard—until she knew without a doubt that he'd found his courage. In her.

Luckily, the president of the campus group stepped forward and started the applause.

Miranda waved one last time, shook hands with the C.I.S.S. president and then accepted Noah's escort down the steps. Before he had a chance to pull her to a private spot, Teri, Katie and a young man who looked a lot like Liam O'Connell, but wasn't, surrounded them.

Miranda pasted on a cordial grin and retreated into that cool, you'll-never-know-what-I'm-really-thinking facade that had waylaid him for so long. Luckily, he now knew better than to buy her nonchalance. Miranda loved him. She'd said so on the beach. She'd intimated her emotions in her very public speech.

Now it was his turn.

The words caught in his throat.

"Noah!" Teri punched him in the arm with all the childlike familiarity of a little sister. He looked at her with surprise. Usually, she was clutching and purring and flirting. "How *courageous* of you to even come tonight, much less interrupt."

"I wouldn't have missed it." He gave Teri a quick

glance, then sought out Miranda's liquid lavender gaze. "Your speech was...enlightening, Miranda."

She glanced down briefly before meeting his stare straight on. "I didn't say anything you don't already know."

"But a lot I haven't been willing to admit."

Katie grabbed her young man by the elbow. "Okay, personal moment. I want to check out the..." She searched the booths and banners for something of interest, her eyes suddenly brightening. "There! A chance to win a romantic evening at a tractor pull. Come on, Sean. Bye, Ms. Carpenter. Dr. C." Her smile turned stony and insistent when she looked at him. "Dr. Yeager."

If ever an expression said *don't blow it*, it was that one.

"Wait," Teri said. "I'll go with you. A tractor pull could be fun. Do they have big brawny men that pull these tractors?"

Their voices faded into the crowd. The bodies milling about melded into a colorful blur along Noah's peripheral vision. He could see only Miranda. She crossed her arms over her chest, enhancing the sweet swell of cleavage her silk tank top afforded. With slim pleated slacks and matching pumps, she wore the palest shade of apricot from her sleeveless blouse to shoes. Her loose blond tresses caressed the curves of her bare shoulders and a chunky gold choker drew his attention to her neck, making his own throat tighten with undeniable desire. She looked professional on the surface, but inherently vulnerable underneath.

She looked exactly how he felt. The parallel threw him off guard.

"Who's that with Katie?" he asked, needing a moment to reform his thoughts.

"Sean O'Connell, Liam's brother. He's a senior creative writing major. Seems Liam decided to play matchmaker to convince Katie that all men aren't dumb."

Noah dug his hands into the pockets of his olive khakis. He really did need to buy an iron. "Judging by my behavior over the past week, I'm not sure that's true."

Miranda murmured her agreement. "I was sort of beginning to wonder myself."

She wove through the crowd, stopping once to make sure Noah followed but glad for the noise and bustle that seemed to offset the quaking throughout her body. With all her heart, she'd hoped he'd come tonight—she'd crafted her speech specifically for him. Yet at the same time, she wished she'd never see him again. Not if it meant not touching him, not kissing him or sharing her most secret thoughts. Desires. Fantasies.

She accepted a free soda from a beer distributor representative, then grabbed one for Noah as well. The carbonated drink brimmed with shaved ice, cooling her throat, but not her belly.

God, she loved him.

"Quite a turnout, huh?" Surrounded by students,

Miranda could do little more than make small talk, as hollow as each word sounded. "There's a band scheduled to go on in an hour if you want to stick around and listen."

"I don't want to listen to any band." He grabbed her by the waist and pulled her forward, spilling some of her soda onto her wrist. Taking the cup, he handed it to the nearest hapless passerby, encircled her wrist with his steely grip and took a lick off her shimmering, sticky skin.

"Noah." Her protest came out only as a whisper. The raspy sound should have died beneath the raucous noise around them, but his eyes darkened as if she'd called out his name in urging rather than in objection. "Everyone will see," she explained.

"Everyone will see what? They'll see what I should have seen a long time ago. I love you, Miranda."

He kissed her wrist, sensually curving his lips to lap up the spilled soda all along the soft skin. He never broke eye contact and Miranda held her breath, willing herself to show no reaction, no response to the confession of his feelings—feelings she'd learned of that night on the beach.

That he loved her wasn't the point. And it wasn't enough.

"I know you love me, Noah. I'm glad you can say it. But it really doesn't change anything, does it?"

Though it broke her heart a second time to do it, she broke his hold and backed away. She was so wrong, so cocky to think she could have a brief fling with Noah, fall in love and then leave. Heartbreak did not make her stronger! She felt certain that if someone bumped into her while she wove her way through the crowd, she'd fall over, get trampled and be happy for it.

A thick wall of students leaping for free T-shirts stopped her escape, allowing Noah the chance to catch up to her. He didn't just grab her hand this time, he wrapped his arm around her middle and nearly carried her away. When he found a secluded spot behind a moving van, he set her down and kissed her, his mouth completely over hers, his arms securely ensnaring her, his body supporting her weight with its full length.

"Don't walk away from me," he begged, his breath stroking her lips, as his kiss had, "ever again. I love you. And not just for today, or next year. I can love you forever. I know that."

Despite the swelling in her heart, despite the tears burning the back of her throat, Miranda was too much a creature of logic to let his declaration go without question. "Why? All these years, you've believed you simply didn't have the capacity to love anyone for the long run. Why am I different?"

She slid her palms over his cheeks, then twined her fingers into his hair. She searched his eyes for an answer, trying not to be soothed into false hopes by the fluid desire that turned his irises to that irresistible shade of midnight blue.

His smile bordered on indulgent, as if the answer was so simple, they were both idiots for not discovering the secret sooner.

"You're different because you know me. You saw right through all the walls I built up. And those were thick walls, sweetheart, because I couldn't even see through them myself until the reality of losing you forced me to knock them down. You fell in love with me, despite the fact that I was—"

He bent his head and winced, then took a deep breath and tried to begin again. She placed the most chaste of kisses on the rugged line of his jaw and soothed the strain from his temples.

"Since you walked away from me at the beach, *physician, heal thyself* kept playing in my mind. I decided a long time ago that I couldn't love anyone, when the fact was, I kept trying to love the wrong women—women who didn't know me any more than I knew them. Not really."

He slid his hands up her back and diminished the hairbreadth of space between them. "But, Miranda, I feel like your soul is so much a part of mine, every new discovery is like a revelation of myself. This connection we have...overwhelmed me, scared the hell out of me." His chuckle sparked a matching reaction in her. They filled the silence with quick laughter, then Miranda watched his face lose all its mirth.

"You spoke about courage and virtue tonight. You were talking right to me, weren't you?"

"I was talking to both of us."

"But only one of us had to come to our senses. Me. Believe me, Miranda, I have. I love you."

He dropped to his knee so fast, Miranda jumped back in surprise. He grabbed both her hands, kissed them—knuckles first, then palms—and gazed up with complete and euphoric surrender.

"Marry me. Be my wife until the day I die."

Miranda swallowed, sure her tongue was too thick to form a word, but she managed to nod. In the morning, she was sure the reality of this would assault her, the magnitude of her agreement would set her heart reeling, but for the moment she wanted nothing but to collapse in his arms.

"Is that a yes?"

She took in another great mouthful of air and pressed her hand, still entwined with his, against her rib cage, as if to force the word out. Not because she didn't want to say it, but because she couldn't believe she was given the chance.

"Yes, Noah. Yes."

Half expecting him to leap up and twirl her around, Miranda watched with wild fascination as his eyelids grew heavy and hooded while he kissed her hands once more. When his mouth began a trail up past her wrists and toward the ultrasensitive crook of her elbows, she glanced around her and pulled back.

"Noah!"

"I'm going to make love to you, Dr./Mrs. Yeager-to-be."

"Not right here," she insisted. "It wasn't easy earning that award. I'd like to keep it for more than ten minutes."

"Why? Aren't you done being a 'good girl'? I'm

quite certain anyone who would marry me doesn't fit the profile."

Miranda grinned and slipped her hands beneath his forearms, urging him to stand up before someone caught them behind the parked truck.

"I'm not a girl anymore, Noah. Haven't been for a while." Slipping her hands around his waist and then sliding them down his taut buttocks, she pressed him close, groaning with pleasure at the feel of his hardening erection against her belly.

"You're not so *good*, either." His hands roamed her body from shoulder to thighs, warming the entire length of her arms, the sensitive sides of her breasts and igniting a thirst she knew only he could quench.

"Oh, yeah? Wanna bet?"

Hooking her hands in his, she stepped backward, drawing him away from the gathering in the center of campus. They were going to make love—that was certain. But Miranda had no intention of doing so anywhere near this crowd.

"Where are you taking me?"

She wiggled her eyebrows, then winked, invigorated by a quickening thrill. She nearly broke into a run, her high heels digging into the soft grassy dirt between the sidewalks. She knew a shortcut.

"Miranda?"

With barely a tug, he yanked her back into his arms and she allowed him to kiss her—briefly. She pulled away, determined to keep this liaison a secret between them, at least for one more night.

He searched her eyes for her intentions, but she

only laughed and urged him to follow her by hooking her fingers into his beltless loops and stepping carefully backward.

"Where are we going?"

"Everyone on campus seems to be at the rally, don't you think?"

Noah glanced over his shoulder. The band, a popular regional group treated to lots of airplay, had just started tuning up. The crowd swelled to easily over five hundred. The campus buildings, spread out over the fifty or so acres that made up the university property, seemed completely devoid of activity.

"Looks that way."

Her lavender eyes lit like amethysts, fired by unadulterated desire. "I doubt anyone would be studying or doing research with all this fun going on..."

Noah needed less than a split second to decipher her suggestion...and no more than five minutes to carry her through the lobby of the library and straight up the staircase to paradise.

Back by popular demand are

DEBBIE MACOMBER's

Hard Luck, Alaska, is a
town that needs women!
And the O'Halloran brothers
are just the fellows
to fly them in.

Starting in March 2000 this beloved series returns
in special 2-in-1 collector's editions:

MAIL-ORDER MARRIAGES, featuring
Brides for Brothers and *The Marriage Risk*
On sale March 2000

FAMILY MEN, featuring
Daddy's Little Helper and *Because of the Baby*
On sale July 2000

THE LAST TWO BACHELORS, featuring
Falling for Him and *Ending in Marriage*
On sale August 2000

Collect and enjoy each MIDNIGHT SONS story!

Available at your favorite retail outlet.

HARLEQUIN®
Makes any time special™

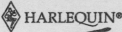

HARLEQUIN®

Temptation®

COMING NEXT MONTH